Lizbeth glanced at the va

Two days ago, selected ~~~ Harvey and herself had been united there, gripped in stasis, allowed to go through limited mitosis. The process had produced a viable embryo—not too common a thing in their world where only a select few were freed of the contraceptive gas and allowed to breed, and only a rare number of those produced viables. She wasn't supposed to understand the intricacies of the process, and the fact that she did understand had to be hidden at all times. *They*—the genetic Optimen of Central—stamped savagely on the slightest threat to their supremacy.

And they considered knowledge in the wrong hands to be the most terrible of threats.

Tor Books by Frank Herbert

THE EYES OF HEISENBERG

FRANK HERBERT

A TOM DOHERTY ASSOCIATES BOOK
NEW YORK

This is a work of fiction. All the characters and events portrayed in this book are either products of the author's imagination or are used fictitiously.

THE EYES OF HEISENBERG

Copyright © 1966, 1994 by Frank Herbert

A Tor Book
Published by Tom Doherty Associates, LLC
175 Fifth Avenue
New York, NY 10010

www.tor.com

Tor® is a registered trademark of Tom Doherty Associates, LLC.

ISBN: 0-765-34252-9

First Tor edition: September 2002

Printed in the United States of America

0 9 8 7 6 5 4 3 2 1

1

They would schedule a rain for this morning, Dr. Thei Svengaard thought. *Rain always makes the parents uneasy . . . not to mention what it does to the doctors.*

A gust of winter wetness rattled against the window behind his desk. He stood, thought of muting the windows, but the Durants—this morning's parents—might be even more alarmed by the unnatural silence on such a day.

Dr. Svengaard stepped to the window, looked down at the thronging foot traffic—day shifts going to their jobs in the megalopolis, night shifts headed toward their tumbled rest. There was a sense of power and movement in the comings and goings of the people in spite of their troglodyte existence. Most of them, he knew, were childless Sterries . . . sterile, sterile. They came and they went, numbered, but numberless.

He had left the intercom open to his reception room and he could hear his nurse, Mrs. Washington, distracting the Durants with questions and forms.

Routine.

That was the watchword. This must all appear normal, casual routine. The Durants and all the others fortunate enough to be chosen *and* to become parents must never suspect the truth.

Dr. Svengaard steered his mind away from such thoughts, reminding himself that guilt was not a permissible emotion for a member of the medical profession. Guilt led inevitably to betrayal . . . and betrayal brought messy consequences. The Optimen were exceedingly touchy where the breeding program was concerned.

Such a thought with its hint of criticism filled Svengaard with a momentary disquiet. He swallowed, allowed his mind to dwell on the Folk response to the Optimen, *They are the power that loves us and cares for us.*

With a sigh, he turned away from the window, skirted the desk and went through the door that led via the ready room to the lab. In the ready room, he paused to check his appearance in the mirror: gray hair, dark brown eyes, strong chin, high forehead and rather grim lips beneath an aquiline nose. He'd always been rather proud of the remote dignity in his appearance-cut and had come to terms with the need of adjusting the remoteness. Now, he softened the set of his mouth, practiced a look of compassionate interest.

Yes, that would do for the Durants—granting the accuracy of their emotional profiles.

Nurse Washington was just ushering the Durants into the lab as Dr. Svengaard entered through his private door. The skylights above them drummed and hissed with the rain. Such weather suddenly seemed to fit the room's mood: washed glass, steel, plasmeld and tile . . . all impersonal. It rained on everyone . . . and all humans had to pass through a room such as this . . . even the Optimen.

Dr. Svengaard took an instant dislike to the parents. Harvey Durant was a lithe six-footer with curly blond hair, light blue eyes. The face was wide with an apparent innocence and youth. Lizbeth, his wife, stood almost the same height, equally blonde, equally blue-eyed and young. Her figure suggested Valkyrie robustness. On a silver cord around her neck she wore one of the omnipresent Folk talismans, a brass figure of the female Optiman, Calapine. The breeder cult nonsense and religious overtones of the figure did not escape Dr. Svengaard. He suppressed a sneer.

The Durants were parents, however, and robust—living

testimony to the skill of the surgeon who had cut them. Dr. Svengaard allowed himself a moment of pride in his profession. Not many people could enter the tight little group of subcellular engineers who kept human variety within bounds.

Nurse Washington paused in the door behind the Durants, said, "Dr. Svengaard, Harvey and Lizbeth Durant." She left without waiting for acknowledgments. Nurse Washington's timing and discretion always were exquisitely correct.

"The Durants, how nice," Dr. Svengaard said. "I hope my nurse didn't bore you with all those forms and questions. But I guess you knew you were letting yourselves in for all that routine when you asked to watch."

"We understand," Harvey Durant said. And he thought, *Asked to watch, indeed! Does this old fake think he can pull his little tricks on us?*

Dr. Svengaard noted the rich, compelling baritone of the man's voice. It bothered him, added to his dislike.

"We don't want to take any more of your time than absolutely necessary," Lizbeth Durant said. She clasped her husband's hand and through their secret code of finger pressures said: *"Do you read him? He doesn't like us."*

Harvey's fingers responded, *"He's a Sterrie prig, so full of pride in his position that he's half blind."*

The woman's no-nonsense tone annoyed Dr. Svengaard. She already was staring around the lab, quick, searching looks. *I must keep control here*, he thought. He crossed to them, shook hands. Their palms were sweaty.

Nervous. Good, Dr. Svengaard thought.

The sound of a viapump at his left seemed reassuringly loud to him then. You could count on the pump to make parents nervous. That was why the pumps were loud. Dr. Svengaard turned toward the sound, indicated a sealed crystal vat on a force-field stand near the lab's center. The pump sound came from the vat.

"Here we are," Dr. Svengaard said.

Lizbeth stared at the vat's milky translucent surface. She wet her lips with her tongue. "In there?"

"And as safe as can be," Dr. Svengaard said.

He cherished the small hope then that the Durants might yet leave, go home and await the outcome.

Harvey took his wife's hand, patted it. He, too, stared at the vat. "We understand you've called in this specialist," he said.

"Dr. Potter," Svengaard said. "From Central." He glanced at the nervous movements of the Durants' hands, noting the omnipresent tattooed index fingers—gene type and station. They could add the coveted "V" for viable now, he thought, and he suppressed a momentary jealousy.

"Dr. Potter, yes," Harvey said. Through their hands, he signaled Lizbeth, *"Notice how he said Central?"*

"How could I miss it?" she responded.

Central, she thought. The place conjured pictures of the lordly Optimen, but this made her think of the Cyborgs who secretly opposed the Optimen, and the whole thing filled her with profound disquiet. She could afford to think of nothing but her son now.

"We know Potter's the best there is," she said. "and we don't want you to think we're just being emotional and fearful . . ."

". . . but we're going to watch," Harvey said. And he thought, *This stiff-necked surgeon had better realize we know our legal rights.*

"I see," Dr. Svengaard said. *Damn these fools!* he thought. But he held his voice to a soothing monotone and said, "Your concern is a matter of record. I admire it. However, the consequences . . ."

He left the words hanging there, reminding them that he had legal rights, too, could make the cut with or without their permission, and couldn't be held responsible for any upset to the parents. Public Law 10927 was clear and direct. Parents might invoke it for the right to watch, but the cut *would* be made at the surgeon's discretion. The human race had a planned future which excluded genetic monsters and wild deviants.

Harvey nodded, a quick and emphatic motion. He gripped his wife's hand tightly. Bits of Folk horror stories and official myths trickled through his mind. He saw Svengaard partly through this confusion of stories and partly through the clandestine forbidden literature grudgingly provided by the Cyborgs to the Parents Underground—through Stedman and Merck, through Shakespeare and Huxley. His youth had fed on such a limited past that he knew superstition could not help but remain.

Lizbeth's nod came slower. She knew what their chief concern here had to be, but that was still her son in the vat.

"Are you sure," she asked, deliberately baiting Svengaard, "that there's no pain?"

The extent of the Folk nonsense which bred in the *necessary* atmosphere of popular ignorance filled Dr. Svengaard with resentment. He knew he'd have to end this interview quickly. The things he *might* be saying to these people kept intruding on his awareness, interfering with what he *had* to say.

"That fertilized ovum has no nerve trains," he said. "It's physically less than three hours old, its growth retarded by controlled nitrate respiration. Pain? The concept doesn't apply."

The technical terms would have little meaning to them, Dr. Svengaard knew, other than to emphasize the distance between mere parents and a submolecular engineer.

"I guess that was rather foolish of me," Lizbeth said. "The . . . it's so simple, not really like a human yet." And she signaled to Harvey through their hands, *"What a simpleton he is! As easy to read as a child."*

Rain beat a tarantella against the skylight. Dr. Svengaard waited it out, then: "Ah, now, let us make no mistakes." And he thought what an excellent moment it was to give these fools a catechism refresher. "Your embryo may be less than three hours old, but it already contains every basic enzyme it'll need when fully developed. An enormously complicated organism."

Harvey stared at him in assumed awe at the *greatness* which could understand such mysteries as the shaping and moulding of life.

Lizbeth glanced at the vat.

Two days ago, selected gametes from Harvey and herself had been united there, gripped in stasis, allowed to go through limited mitosis. The process had produced a viable embryo—not too common a thing in their world where only a select few were freed of the contraceptive gas and allowed to breed, and only a rare number of those produced viables. She wasn't supposed to understand the intricacies of the process, and the fact that she did understand had to be hidden at all times. *They*—the genetic Optimen of Central—stamped savagely on the slightest threat to their supremacy. And *they* considered knowledge in the wrong hands to be the most terrible threat.

"How . . . big is . . . he now?" she asked.

"Diameter less than a tenth of a millimeter," Dr. Svengaard said. He relaxed his face into a smile. "It's a morula and back in the primitive days it wouldn't yet have completed its journey to the uterus. This is the stage when it's most susceptible to us. We must do our work now before the formation of the trophoblast."

The Durants nodded in awe.

Dr. Svengaard basked in their respect. He sensed their minds fumbling over poorly remembered definitions from the limited schooling they'd been permitted. Their records said she was a creche librarian and he an instructor of the young—not much education required for either.

Harvey touched the vat, jerked his hand away. The crystal surface felt warm, filled with subtle vibrations. And there was that constant *thrap-thrap-thrap* of the pump. He sensed the deliberateness of that annoying sound, reading the way he'd been trained in the Underground the subtle betrayals in Svengaard's manner. He glanced around the laboratory—glass pipes, square gray cabinets, shiny angles and curves of plasmeld, omnipresent gauges like staring eyes. The place smelled of disinfectants and exotic chemicals. Everything about the lab carried that calculated double purpose—functional yet designed to awe the uninitiated.

Lizbeth focused on the one mundane feature of the place she could really recognize for certain—a tile sink with gleaming faucets. The sink sat squeezed between two mysterious constructions of convoluted glass and dull gray plasmeld.

The sink bothered Lizbeth. It represented a place of disposal. You flushed garbage into a sink for grinding before it was washed into the sewage reclamation system. Anything small could be dumped into a sink and lost.

Forever.

Anything.

"I'm not going to be talked out of watching," she said.

Damn! Dr. Svengaard thought. *There was a catch in her voice.* That little catch, that hesitation was betrayal. It didn't fit with her bold appearance. Overemphasis on maternal drive in her cutting . . . no matter how successful the surgeon had been with the rest of her.

"Our concern is for you as much as for your child," Dr. Svengaard said. "The trauma . . ."

"The law gives us the right," Harvey said. And he signaled to Lizbeth, *"The whole pattern's more or less what we anticipated."*

Trust this clod to know the law, Dr. Svengaard thought. He sighed. Statistical prediction said one in one hundred thousand parents would insist, despite all the subtle and not so subtle pressures against it. Statistics and visible fact, however, were two distinct matters. Svengaard had noted how Harvey glared at him. The man's cutting had been strong on male protectiveness—too strong, obviously. He couldn't stand to see his *mate* thwarted. Doubtless he was an excellent provider, model husband, never participated in Sterrie orgies—a leader.

A clod.

"The law," Dr. Svengaard said, and his voice dripped rebuke, "also requiries that I point out the dangers of psychological trauma to the parents. I was *not* suggesting I'd try to prevent you from watching."

"We're going to watch," Lizbeth said.

Harvey felt a surge of admiration for her then. She played her role so beautifully, even to that catch in her voice.

"I couldn't stand the waiting otherwise," Lizbeth said. "Not knowing . . ."

Dr. Svengaard wondered if he dared press the matter—perhaps an appeal to their obvious awe, a show of Authority. One look at Harvey's squared shoulders and Lizbeth's pleading eyes dissuaded him. They were going to watch.

"Very well," Dr. Svengaard sighed.

"Will we watch from here?" Harvey asked.

Dr. Svengaard was shocked. "Of course not!" What primitives, these clods. But he tempered the thought with realization that such ignorance resulted from the carefully fostered mystery that surrounded gene shaping. In a calmer tone, he said, "You'll have a private room with a closed-circuit connection to this lab. My nurse will escort you."

Nurse Washington proved her competence then by appearing in the doorway. She'd been listening, of course. A good nurse never left such matters to chance.

"Is this all we get to see here?" Lizbeth asked.

Dr. Svengaard heard the pleading tone, noted the way she avoided looking directly at the vat. All his pent-up scorn came out in his voice as he said, "What else is there to see, Mrs. Durant? Surely you didn't expect to see the morula."

Harvey tugged at his wife's arm, said, "Thank you, Doctor."

Once more, Lizbeth's eyes scanned the room, avoiding the vat. "Yes, thank you for showing us . . . this room. It helps to see how . . . prepared you are for . . . every emergency." Her eyes focused on the sink.

"You're quite welcome, I'm sure," Dr. Svengaard said. "Nurse Washington will provide you with the list of permissible names. You might occupy part of your time choosing a name for your son if you've not already done so." He nodded to the nurse. "See the Durants to Lounge Five, please."

Nurse Washington said, "If you'll follow me, please?" She turned with that air of overworked impatience which Svengaard suspected all nurses acquired with their diplomas. The Durants were sucked up in her wake.

Svengaard turned back to the vat.

So much to do—Potter, the specialist from Central, due within the hour . . . and he wouldn't be happy about the Durants. People had so little understanding of what the medical profession endured. The psychological preparation of parents subtracted from time better devoted to more important matters . . . and it certainly complicated the security problem. Svengaard thought of the five "Destroy After Reading" directives he'd received from Max Allgood, Central's boss of T-Security, during the past month. It was disturbing, as though some new danger had set Security scurrying.

But Central insisted on the socializing with parents. The Optimen must have good reason, Svengaard felt. Most things *they* did made wonderful sense. Sometimes, Svengaard knew, he fell into a feeling of orphanage, a creature without past. All it took to shake him from the emotional morass, though, was a moment's contemplation: *"They are the power that loves us and cares for us."* *They* had the world firmly in their grip, the future planned—a place for every man and every man in his place. Some of the old dreams—space travel, the questing philosophies, farming of the seas—had been shelved temporarily, put aside for more important things. The day would come, though, once *they* solved the unknowns behind submolecular engineering.

Meanwhile, there was work for the willing—maintaining the population of workers, suppressing deviants, husbanding the genetic pool from which even the Optimen sprang.

Svengaard swung the meson microscope over the Durant vat, adjusted for low amplification to minimize Heisenberg interference. One more look wouldn't hurt, just on the chance he might locate the pilot-cell and reduce Potter's problem. Even as he bent to the scope, Svengaard knew he was rationalizing. He couldn't resist another search into this morula which had the potential, might be shaped into an Optiman. The wonderous things were so rare. He flicked the switch, focused.

A sigh escaped him, "Ahhhhh . . ."

So passive the morula at low amplification; no pulsing as it lay within the stasis—yet so beautiful in its semidormancy . . . so little to hint that it was the arena of ancient battles.

Svengaard put a hand to the amplification controls, hesitated. High amplification posed its dangers, but Potter could re-adjust minor marks of meson interference. And the *big* look was very tempting.

He doubled amplification.

Again.

Enlargement always reduced the appearance of stasis. Things moved here, and in the unfocused distances there were flashes like the dartings of fish. Up cut of the swarming arena came the triple spiral of nucleotides that had led him to call Potter. Almost Optiman. Almost that beautiful perfection of form and mind that could accept the indefinite balancing of Life through the delicately adjusted enzyme prescriptions.

A sense of loss pervaded Svengaard. His own prescription, while it kept him alive, was slowly killing him. It was the fate of all men. They might live two hundred years, sometimes even more . . . but in the end the balancing act failed for all except the Optimen. They were perfect, limited only by their physical sterility, but that was the fate of many humans and it subtracted nothing from endless life.

His own childless state gave Svengaard a sense of communion with the Optimen. *They'd* solve that, too . . . someday.

He concentrated on the morula. A sulfur-containing amino acid dependency showed faint motion at this amplification. With a feeling of shock, Svengaard recognized it—isovalthine, a genetic marker for latent myxedema, a warning of potential thyroid deficiency. It was a disquieting flaw in the otherwise near-perfection. Potter would have to be alerted.

Svengaard backed off amplification to study the mitochondrial structure. He followed out the invaginated unit-membrane to the flattened, sac-like cristae, returned along the external second membrane, focused on the hydrophilic outer compartment. Yes . . . the isovalthine was susceptible to adjustment. Perfection might yet be for this morula.

Flickering movement appeared at the edge of the microscope's field.

Svengaard stiffened, thought, *Dear God, no!*

He stood frozen at the viewer as a thing seen only eight previous times in the history of gene-shaping took place within his field of vision.

A thin line like a distant contrail reached into the cellular structure from the left. It wound through a coiled-coil of alpha helices, found the folded ends of the polypeptide chains in a myosin molecule, twisted and dissolved.

Where the trail had been now lay a new structure about four Angstroms in diameter and a thousand Angstroms long—sperm protamine rich in arginine. All around it the protein factories of the cytoplasm were undergoing change, fighting the stasis, realigning. Svengaard recognized what was happening from the descriptions of the eight previous occurrences. The ADP-ATP exchange system was becoming more complex—"resistant." The surgeon's job had been made infinitely more complex.

Potter will be furious, Svengaard thought.

Svengaard turned off the microscope, straightened. He wiped perspiration from his hands, glanced at the lab clock. Less than two minutes had passed. The Durants weren't even in their lounge yet. But in those two minutes, some force . . . some energy from *outside* had made a seemingly purposeful adjustment within the embryo.

Could this be what's stirred up Security . . . and the Optimen? Svengaard wondered.

He had heard this thing described, read the reports . . . but actually to have seen it himself! To have seen it . . . so sure and purposeful . . .

He shook his head. *No! It was not purposeful! It was merely an accident, chance, nothing more.*

But the vision wouldn't leave him.

Compared to that, he thought, *how clumsy my efforts are. And I'll have to report it to Potter. He'll have to shape that twisted chain . . . if he can now that it's resistant.*

Full of disquiet, not at all satisfied that he had seen an accident, Svengaard began making the final checks of the lab's preparations. He inspected the enzyme racks and their linkage to the computer dosage-control—plenty of cyto-chrome b_5 and P-450 hemoprotein, a good reserve store of ubiquinone and sulfhydryl, arsenate, azide and oligomycin, sufficient protein-bound phosphohistidine. He moved down the line—acylating agents, a store of (2,4-dinitrophenol) and the isoxazolidon-3 groups with reduction NADH.

He turned to the physical equipment, checked the meson scalpel's micromechanism, read the life-system gauges on the vat and the print-out of the stasis mechanism.

All in order.

It had to be. The Durant embryo, that beautiful thing with its wondrous potential, was now *resistant*—a genetic un-known . . . if Potter could succeed where others had failed.

2

Dr. Vyaslav Potter stopped at the Records Desk on his way into the hospital. He was faintly tired after the long tube-shunt from Central to Seatac Megalopolis, still he told an off-color joke about primitive reproduction to the gray-haired duty nurse. She chuckled as she hunted up Svengaard's latest report on the Durant embryo. She put the report on the counter and stared at Potter.

He glanced at the folder's cover and looked up to meet the nurse's eyes.

Is it possible? he wondered. *But . . . no: she's too old— wouldn't even make a good playmate. Anyway, the big-domes wouldn't grant us a breeding permit.* And he reminded himself: I'm a Zeek . . . J^411118^2K. The Zeek gene-shaping had gone through a brief popularity in the region of Timbuctu Megalopolis during the early nineties. It produced curly black hair, a skin one shade lighter than milk chocolate, soft brown eyes and a roly-poly face of utmost benignity, all on a tall, strong body. A Zeek. A Vyaslav Potter.

It had yet to produce an Optiman, male or female, and never a viable gamete match.

Potter had long since given up. He was one of those who'd voted to discontinue the Zeek. He thought of the

Optimen with whom he dealt and sneered at himself, *There but for the brown eyes* . . . But the sneer no longer gave him a twinge of bitterness.

"You know," he said, smiling at the nurse, "these Durants whose emb I have this morning—I cut them both. Maybe I've been in this business too long."

"Oh, go on with you, Doctor," she said with an arch turn of her head. "You're not even middle-aged. You don't look a day over a hundred."

He glanced at the folder. "But here are these kids bringing me their emb to cut and I . . ." He shrugged.

"Are you going to tell them?" she asked. "I mean that you had them, too."

"I probably won't even see them," he said. "You know how it is. Anyway, sometimes people are happy with their cut . . . sometimes they wish they'd had a little more of this, less of that. They tend to blame the surgeon. They don't understand, *can't* understand the problems we have in the cutting room."

"But the Durants seem like a very successful cut," she said. "Normal, happy . . . perhaps a little over-worried about their son, but . . ."

"Their genotype is one of the most successful," he said. He tapped the record folder with a forefinger. "Here's the proof: they had a viable with potential." He lifted a thumb in the time-honored gesture for Optiman.

"You should be very proud of them," she said. "My family's had only fifteen viables in a hundred and eighty-nine years, and never an . . ." She repeated Potter's thumb gesture.

He pursed his lips into a moue of commiseration, wondering how he let himself get drawn into these conversations with women, especially with nurses. It was that little seed of hope that never died, he suspected. It was cut from the same stuff that produced the wild rumors, the quack "breeder doctors" and the black market in "true breed" nostrums. It was the thing that sold the little figurines of Optiman-Calapine because of the unfounded rumor that she had produced a viable. It was the thing that wore out the big toes of fertility idols from the kisses of the hopeful.

His moue of commiseration became a cynical sneer. *Hopeful! If they only knew.*

"Were you aware the Durants are going to watch?" the nurse asked.

His head jerked up and he glared at her.

"It's all over the hospital," she said. "Security's been alerted. The Durants have been scanned and they're in Lounge Five with closed circuit to the cutting room."

Anger blazed through him. "Damn it to hell! Can't they do anything right in this stupid place?"

"Now, Doctor," she said, stiffening into the prim departmental dictator. "There's no call to lose your temper. The Durants quoted the law. That ties our hands and you know it."

"Stupid damn' law," Potter muttered, but his anger had subsided. *The law!* he thought. *More of the damn' masquerade.* He had to admit, though, that they needed the law. Without Public Law 10927, people might ask the wrong kinds of questions. And no doubt Svengaard had done his bumbling best to try to dissuade the Durants.

Potter assumed a rueful grin, said, "Sorry I snapped like that. I've had a bad week." He sighed. "They just don't understand."

"Is there any other record you wish, Doctor?" she asked.

Rapport was gone, Potter saw. "No, thanks," he said. He took the Durant folder, headed for Svengaard's office. Just his luck: a pair of watchers. It meant plenty of extra work. Naturally!

The Durants couldn't be content with seeing the tape *after* the cut. Oh, no. *They* had to be on the scene. That meant the Durants weren't as innocent as they might appear—no matter what this hospital's Security staff said. The public just did not insist anymore. That was supposed to have been *cut* out of them.

The statistical few who defied their genetic shaping now required special attention.

And Potter reminded himself, *I did the original cut on this pair. There was no mistake.*

He ran into Svengaard outside the latter's office, heard the man's quick résumé. Svengaard then began babbling about his Security arrangments.

"I don't give a damn what your Security people say," Potter barked. "We've new instructions. Central Emergency's to be called in every case of this kind."

They went into Svengaard's office. It pretended to wood paneling—a corner room with a view of flowered roof gardens and terraces built of the omnipresent three-phase regenerative plasmeld, the "plasty" of the Folk patios. Nothing must age or degenerate in this best of all Optiman worlds. Nothing except people.

"Central Emergency?" Svengaard asked.

"No exceptions," Potter said. He sat in Svengaard's chair, put his feet on Svengaard's desk, and brought the little ivory-colored phone box to his stomach with its screen only inches from his face. He punched in Security's number and his own code identification.

Svengaard sat on a corner of the desk across from him, appearing both angry and cowed. "They were scanned, I tell you," he said. "They were carrying no unusual devices. There's nothing unusual about them."

"Except they insist on watching," Potter said. He jiggled the phone key. "What's keeping those ignoramuses?"

Svengaard said, "But the law—"

"Damn the law!" Potter said. "You know as well as I do that we could route the view signal from the cutting room through an editing computer and show the parents anything we want. Has it ever occurred to you to wonder why we don't do just that?"

"Why . . . they . . . ahh . . ." Svengaard shook his head. The question had caught him off balance. Why wasn't that done? The statistics showed a certain number of parents would insist on watching and . . .

"It was tried," Potter said. "Somehow, the parents detected the computer's hand in the tape."

"How?"

"We don't know."

"Weren't the parents questioned and . . ."

"They killed themselves."

"Killed them—How?"

"We don't know."

Svengaard tried to swallow in a dry throat. He began to get a picture of intense excitement just under Security's surface. He said, "What about the statistical ratio of—"

"Statistical, my ass!" Potter said.

A heavy masculine voice came from the phone: "Who're you talking to?"

Potter focused on the screen, said, "I was talking to Sven. This viable he called me on—"

"It is a viable?"

"Yes! It's a viable with the full potential, but the parents insist on watching the—"

"I'll have a full crew on the way by tube in ten minutes," said the voice on the phone. "They're at Friscopolis. Shouldn't take 'em more than a few minutes."

Svengaard rubbed wet palms against the sides of his working smock. He couldn't see that face on the phone, but the voice sounded like Max Allgood, T Security's boss.

"We'll delay the cut until your people get here," Potter said. "The records are being faxed to you and should be on your desk in a few minutes. There's another—"

"Is that embryo everything we were told?" asked the man on the phone. "Any flaws?"

"A latent myxedema, a projective faulty heart valve, but the—"

"Okay, I'll call you after I've seen the—"

"Damn it to hell!" Potter erupted. "Will you let me get ten words out of my mouth without interrupting?" He glared into the screen. "There's something here more important than flaw and the parents." Potter glanced up at Svengaard, back to the screen. "Sven reports he saw an *outside* adjustment of the arginine deficiency."

A low whistle came from the phone, then, "Reliable?"

"Depend on it."

"Did it follow the pattern of the other eight?"

Potter glanced up at Svengaard, who nodded.

"Sven says yes."

"*They* won't like that."

"*I* don't like it."

"Did Sven see enough to get any . . . new ideas on it?"

Svengaard shook his head.

"No," Potter said.

"There's a strong possibility it isn't significant," the man on the phone said. "In a system of increasing determinism—"

"Oh, yes," Potter sneered. "In a system of increasing determinism you get more and more indeterminism. You might as well say in a foofram of increasing haggersmaggle—"

"Well, it's what *they* believe."

"So they say. *I* believe Nature doesn't like being meddled with."

Potter stared into the screen. For some reason, he recalled his youth, the beginning of his medical studies and the day he'd learned how *very* close his genotype had been to the Optiman. He found that the old core of hatred had become mildly amused tolerance and cynicism.

"I don't see why they put up with you," the man on the phone said.

"Because I was *very* close," Potter whispered. He wondered then how close the Durant embryo would be. *I'll do my best*, he thought.

The man on the phone cleared his throat, said, "Yes, well I'll depend on you to handle things at your end. The embryo ought to provide some verification of the outside inter—"

"Don't be a total ass!" Potter snapped. "The emb will bear out Sven's report to the last enzyme. You tend to your job; we'll do ours." He slapped the cut-off, pushed the phone back onto the desk and sat staring at it. "Pompous damned . . . no—he's what he is because he's what he is. Comes from living too close to *them*. Comes from the original cut. Maybe I'd be an ass too if that's what I had to be."

Svengaard tried to swallow in a dry throat. He'd never before heard such an argument or such frank talk from the men who operated out of Central.

"Shocked you, eh, Sven?" Potter asked. He dropped his feet to the floor.

Svengaard shrugged. He felt ill-at-ease.

Potter studied the man. Svengaard was good within his limits, but he lacked creative imagination. A brilliant surgeon, but without that special quality he was often a dull tool.

"You're a good man, Sven," Potter said. "Dependable. That's what your record says, you know. Dependable. You'll never be anything else. Weren't meant to be. In your particular niche, though, you're *it*."

Svengaard heard only the praise, said, "It's good to be appreciated, of course, but—"

"But we have work to do."

"It will be difficult," Svengaard said. "Now."

"Do you think that *outside* adjustment was an accidental thing?" Potter asked.

"I—I'd like to believe that"—Svengaard wet his lips with his tongue—"it wasn't *determined*, that no agency . . ."

"You'd like to lay it to uncertainty, to Heisenberg," Potter said. "The principle of uncertainty, some result of our own meddling—everything an accident in the capricious universe."

Svengaard felt stung by a quality of harshness in Potter's voice, said, "Not precisely. I meant only that I hoped no super causal agency had a hand in—"

"God? You don't really mean you're afraid this is the action of a deity?"

Svengaard looked away. "I remember in school," he said. "You were lecturing. You said we always have to be ready to face the fact that the reality we see will be shockingly different from anything our theories led us to suspect."

"Did I say that? Did I really say that?"

"You did."

"Something's out there, eh? Something beyond our instruments. It's never heard of Heisenberg. It isn't uncertain at all. It moves." His voice lowered. "It moves directly. It

adjusts things." He cocked his head to one side. "Ah-hah!
The ghost of Heisenberg is confounded!"

Svengaard glared at Potter. The man was mocking him.
He spoke stiffly, "Heisenberg did point out that we have
our limits."

"You're right," Potter said. "There's a caprice in our universe. He taught us that. There's always something we can't
interpret or understand . . . or measure. He set us up for this
present dilemma, eh?" Potter glanced at his finger watch,
back to Svengaard. "We tend to interpret everything around
us by screening it through that system which is native to
us. Our civilization sees indeterminately through the eyes
of Heisenberg. If he taught us truly, how can we tell
whether the unknown's an accident or the deliberate intent
of God? What's the use of even asking?"

Svengaard spoke defensively, "We appear to manage,
somehow."

Potter startled him by laughing, head tipped back, body
shaking with enjoyment. The laughter subsided and presently Potter said, "Sven, you are a gem. I mean that. If it
weren't for the ones like you, we'd still be back in the muck
and mire, running from glaciers and saber-tooth tigers."

Svengaard fought to keep anger from his voice, said,
"What do *they* think this arginine adjustment is?"

Potter stared at him, measuring, then, "Damned if I
haven't underestimated you, Sven. Apologies, eh?"

Svengaard shrugged. Potter was acting oddly today—
astonishing reactions, strange eruptions of emotion. "Do
you *know* what they say about this?" he asked.

"You heard Max on the phone," Potter said.

So that was Allgood, Svengaard thought.

"Certainly, I know," Potter growled. "Max has it all
wrong. *They* say gene-shaping inflicts itself on nature—on
a nature that can never be reduced to mechanical systems
and, therefore, to stationary matter. You can't stop the
movement, see? It's an extended system phenomenon, energy seeking a level that's—"

"Extended system?" Svengaard asked.

Potter looked up at the man's scowling face. The question focused Potters' attention abruptly on the differences in thought patterns between those who lived close to Central and those who touched the Optiman world only through reports and second-hand associations.

We are so different, Potter thought. *Just as the Optimen are different from us and Sven here is different from the Sterries and breeders. We're cut off from each other . . . and none of us has a past. Only the Optimen have a past. But each has an individual past . . . selfishly personal . . . and ancient.*

"Extended system," Potter said. "From the microcosmos to the macrocosmos, *they* say all is order and systems. The *idea* of matter is insubstantial. All is collisions of energy— some appearing large, swift and spectacular . . . some small, gentle and slow. But this too is relative. The aspects of energy are infinite. Everything depends on the viewpoint of the observer. For each change of viewpoint, the energy rules change. There exist an infinite number of energy rules, each set dependent on the twin aspects of viewpoint and background. In an extended system, this *thing* from outside assumes the aspect of a node appearing on a standing wave. That's what *they* say."

Svengaard slipped off the desk, stood in a rapture of awe. He felt that he'd had a fleeting glimpse, a wisp of understanding that penetrated every question he might ask about the universe.

Could that be what it's like to work out of Central? he wondered.

"That's a great summation, isn't it?" Potter demanded. He stood up. "A truly *great* idea!" A chuckle shook him.

"You know, a guy named Diderot had that idea. It was around 1750 or thereabout. *They* spoon-feed it to us now. Great wisdom!"

"Maybe Diderot was . . . one of *them*," Svengaard ventured.

Potter sighed, thinking, *How ignorant a man can become on a diet of managed history.* He wondered then how his own diet had been adjusted and managed.

"Diderot was one of us," Potter growled.

Svengaard stared at him, shocked to silence by the man's . . . blasphemy.

"It comes down to this," Potter said. "Nature doesn't like being meddled with."

A chime sounded beneath Svengaard's desk.

"Security?" Potter asked.

"That's the all clear," Svengaard said. "They're ready for us now."

"Central's Security hotshots are all in place," Potter said. "You will note that they didn't stoop to report to you or to me. They watch us too, you know."

"I've . . . nothing to hide," Svengaard said.

"Of course you haven't," Potter said. He moved around the desk, threw an arm across Svengaard's shoulders. "Come along. It's time for us to put on the mask of Archeus. We're going to give form and organization to a living body. Veritable gods, we are."

Svengaard felt himself still lost in confusion. "What'll *they* do . . . to the Durants?" he asked.

"Do? Not a damn' thing—unless the Durants force it. The Durants won't even know they're being watched. But Central's little boys will know everything that goes on in that lounge. The Durants won't be able to belch without the gas being subjected to a full and complete analysis. Come along."

But Svengaard held back. "Doctor Potter," he asked, "what do *you* think introduced that arginine chain into the Durant morula?"

"I'm closer to you than you think," Potter said. "We're fighting . . . instability. We've upset the biological stability of the inheritance patterns with our false isomers and our enzyme adjustments and our meson beams. We've undermined the chemical stability of the molecules in the germ plasm. You're a doctor. Look at the enzyme prescriptions we all have to take—how profound the adjustment we have to make to stay alive. It wasn't always that way. And *whatever* set up that original stability is still in there fighting. *That's* what I think."

3

The cutting room nurses positioned the vat under the enzyme console, readied the tubes and the computer-feed-analysis board. They worked quietly, efficiently as Potter and Svengaard examined the gauges. The computer nurse racked her tapes and there came a brief whirring-clicking as she tested her board.

Potter felt himself filled with the wakeful anxiety that always came over him before surgery. He knew it would give way presently to the charged sureness of action, but he felt snappish at the moment. He glanced at the vat gauges. The Krebs cycle was holding at 86.9, a good sixty points above death level. The vat nurse came over, examined his breather mask. He checked his microphone, "Mary had a little lamb, its fleece was black as hades—the surgeon took the credit for . . . a joke on all the ladies."

He heard a distinct chuckle from the computer nurse, glanced at her, but she had her back to him and her face already hidden by hood and mask.

The vat nurse said, "Microphone working, Doctor."

He couldn't see her lips moving behind her mask, but her cheeks rippled as she spoke.

Svengaard flexed his fingers in their gloves, took a deep breath. It smelled faintly of ammonia. He wondered why

Potter always joked with the nurses. It seemed demeaning, somehow.

Potter moved across to the vat. His sterile suit crinkled with a familiar snapping hiss as he walked. He glanced up at the wall screen, the replay monitor which showed approximately what the surgeon saw and which was the view watched by the parents. The screen presented him with a view of itself as he turned his forehead pickup lens toward it.

Damn' parents, he thought. *They make me feel guilty . . . all of them.*

He returned his attention to the crystal vat now bristling with instruments. The pump's churgling annoyed him.

Svengaard moved to the other side of the vat, waiting. The breather mask hid the lower half of his face, but his eyes appeared calm. He radiated a sense of steadiness, reliability.

How does he really feel? Potter wondered. And he reminded himself that in an emergency there wasn't a better cutting-room assistant than Sven.

"You can begin increasing the pyruvic acid," Potter said.

Svengaard nodded, depressed the feeder key.

The computer nurse started her reels turning.

They watched the gauges as the Krebs cycle began rising—87.0 . . . 87.3 . . . 87.8 . . . 88.5 . . . 89.4 . . . 90.5 . . . 91.9 . . .

Now, Potter told himself, *the irreversible movement of growth has started. Only death can stop it.* "Tell me when the Krebs cycle reaches one hundred and ten," he said.

He swung the scope and micromanipulators into place, leaned into the rests. *Will I see what Sven saw?* he wondered. He knew it wasn't likely. The lightning from *outside* had never struck twice in the same place. It came. It did what no human hand could do. It went away.

Where? Potter wondered.

The inter-ribosomal gaps swam into focus. He scanned them, boosted amplification and went down into the DNA spirals. Yes—there was the situation Sven had described. The Durant embryo was one of those that could cross over into the more-than-human land of Central . . . if the surgeon succeeded.

The confirmation left Potter oddly shaken. He shifted his attention to the mitochondrial structures, saw the evidence of the arginine intrusion. It squared precisely with Sven's description. Alpha-helices had begun firming up, revealing the telltale striations at the aneurin shifts. This one was going to resist the surgeon. This was going to be a tough one.

Potter straightened.

"Well?" Svengaard asked.

"Pretty much as you described it," Potter said. "A straightforward job." That was for the watching parents.

He wondered then what Security was discovering about the Durants. Would this pair be loaded down with search and probe devices disguised as conventional artifacts? Possibly. But there were rumors of new techniques being introduced by the Parents Underground . . . and of Cyborgs moving out of the dark shadows which had hidden them for centuries—if there were Cyborgs at all. Potter was not convinced.

Svengaard spoke to the computer nurse, "Start backing off the pyruvic."

"Backing off pyruvic," she said.

Potter swung his attention to the priority rack beside him, checked the presentation—in the first row the pyrimidines, nucleic acids and proteins, then aneurin, riboflavin, pyridoxin, pantothenic acid, folic acid, choline, inositol, sulfhydryl . . .

He cleared his throat, lining up his plan for the attack on the morula's defenses. "I will attempt to find a pilot cell by masking the cysteine at a single locus," he said. "Stand by with sulfhydryl and prepare an intermediary tape for protein synthesis."

"Ready for masking," Svengaard said. He nodded to the computer nurse who racked the intermediary tape into position with a smooth sureness.

"Krebs cycle?" Potter asked.

"One hundred and ten coming up," Svengaard said.

Silence.

"Mark," Svengaard said.

Again, Potter bent to the scope. "Begin the tape," he said. "Two minims of sulfhydryl."

Slowly, Potter increased amplification, chose a cell for the masking. The momentary clouding of intrusion cleared away and he searched the surrounding cells for clues that mitosis would take off on his *directed* tangent. It was slow . . . slow. He'd just begun and his hands already felt sweaty in their gloves.

"Stand by with adenosine triphosphate," he said.

Svengaard presented the feeder tube in the micromanip-ulators, nodded to the vat nurse. ATP already. This was going to be a tough one.

"Begin one minim ATP," Potter said.

Svengaard depressed the feeder key. The whirring of the computer tapes sounded overly loud.

Potter lifted his head momentarily, shook it. "Wrong cell," he said. "We'll try another one. Same procedure." Again, he leaned into the scope and the rests, moved the micromanipulators, pushing amplification up a notch at a time. Slowly, he traced his way down into the cellular mass. *Gently . . . gently . . .* The scope itself could cause irrevers-ible damage in here.

Ahhh, he thought, recognizing an active cell deep in the morula. Vat-stasis had produced only a relative slowing in here. The cell was the scene of intense chemical activity. He recognized doubled base pairs strung on a convoluted helix of sugar phosphate as they passed his field of vision.

His beginning anxiety had passed and he felt the old sureness with the often repeated sensation that the morula was an ocean in which he swam, that the cellular interior was his natural habitat.

"Two minims of sulfhydryl," Potter said.

"Sulfhydryl, two minims," Svengaard said. "Standing by with ATP."

"ATP," Potter said, then, "I'm going to inhibit the exchange reaction in the mitochondrial systems. Start oli-gomycin and azide."

Svengaard proved his worth then by complying without hesitation. The only sign that he recognized the dangers in this procedure was a question, "Shall I have an uncoupling agent ready?"

"Stand by with arsenate in number one," Potter said.

"Krebs cycle going down," the computer nurse said. "Eighty-nine point four."

"Intrusion effect," Potter said. "Give me point six minim of azide."

Svengaard depressed the key.

"Point four minim oligomycin," Potter said.

"Oligomycin, point four," Svengaard said.

Potter felt that he lived now only through his eyes on the microscope and his hands on the micromanipulators. His existence had moved into the morula, fused with it.

His eyes told him that peripheral mitosis had stopped . . . as it should under these ministrations. "I *think* we have it," he said. He planted a marker on the scope position, shifted focus and went down into the DNA spirals, seeking the hydroxyl deformity, the flaw that would produce a faulty heart valve. Now he was the artist, the master cutter—the pilot cell determined. Now he moved to reshape the delicate chemical factory of the inner structure.

"Prepare for the cut," he said.

Svengaard armed the meson generator. "Armed," he said.

"Krebs cycle seventy-one," the computer nurse said.

"First cut," Potter said. He let off the single, aimed burst, watched the tumbling chaos that followed. The hydroxyl appendage vanished. Nucleotides reformed.

"Hemoprotein P-450," Potter said. "Stand by to reduce it with NADH." He waited, studying the globular proteins that formed before him, watching for biologically active molecules. *Now!* Instinct and training combined to tell him the precise instant. "Two and a half minims of P-450," he said.

A corner of turmoil engaged a group of polypeptide chains in the heart of the cell.

"Reduce it," Potter said.

Svengaard touched the NADH feeder key. He couldn't

see what Potter saw, but the surgeon's forehead lens repro-
duced a slightly off-parallax view of the scope field. That
plus Potter's instructions told of the slow spread of change
in the cell.

"Krebs cycle fifty-eight," the computer nurse said.

"Second cut," Potter said.

"Armed," Svengaard said.

Potter searched out the myxedema-latent isovaithine,
found it. "Give me a tape on structure," he said. "S-
(isopropylcarboxymethyl) cystein."

Computer tape hissed through the reels, stopped, re-
sumed at a slow, steady pace. The isovaltine comparison
image appeared in the upper right quadrant of Potter's
scope field. He compared the structures, point for point,
said, "Tape off." The comparison image vanished.

"Krebs cycle forty-seven," the computer nurse said.

Potter took a deep, trembling breath. Another twenty-
seven points and they'd be in the death range. The Durant
embryo would succumb.

He swallowed, aimed off the meson burst.

Isovalthine tumbled apart.

"Ready with cycloserine," Svengaard said.

Ahhh, good old Sven, Potter thought. *You don't have to
tell him every step of the way what to do.*

"Comparison on D-4-aminoisoxazolidon-3," Potter said.

The computer nurse readied the tape, said, "Comparison
ready."

The comparison image appeared in Potter's view field.
"Check," he said. The image vanished. "One point eight
minims." He watched the interaction of the enzymic func-
tional groups as Svengaard administered the cycloserine.
The amino group showed a nice, open field of affinity.
Transfer-RNA fitted readily into its niches.

"Krebs cycle thirty-eight point six," the computer nurse
said.

We'll have to chance it, Potter thought. *This embryo
won't take more adjustment.*

"Reduce vat stasis to half," he said. "Increase ATP. Give
me micro-feed on ten minims of pyruvic acid."

"Reducing stasis," Svengaard said. And he thought, *This will be close*. He keyed the ATP and pyruvic acid feeders.

"Give me the Krebs cycle on the half point," Potter said.

"Thirty-five," the nurse said. "Thirty-four point five. Thirty-four. Thirty-three point five." Her voice picked up speed with a shocked breathlessness: "Thirty-three . . . thirty-two . . . thirty-one . . . thirty . . . twenty-nine . . ."

"Release all stasis," Potter said. "Present the full amino spectrum with activated histidine. Start pyridoxin—four point two minims."

Svengaard's hands sped over the keys.

"Back-feed the protein tape," Potter ordered. "Give it the full DNA record on computer automatic."

Tapes hissed through the reels.

"It's slowing," Svengaard said.

"Twenty-two," the computer nurse said. "Twenty-one nine . . . twenty-two . . . twenty-one nine . . . twenty-two one . . . twenty-two two . . . twenty-two one . . . twenty two two . . . twenty-two three . . . twenty-two four . . . twenty-two three . . . twenty-two four . . . twenty-two five . . . twenty-two six . . . twenty-two five . . ."

Potter felt the see-saw battle through every nerve. The morula was down at the edge of the death range. It could live or it could die in the next few minutes. Or it could come out of this crippled. Such things happened. When the flaw was too gross, the vat was turned off, flushed out. But Potter felt an identification with this embryo now. He felt he couldn't afford to lose it.

"Mutagen desensitizer," he said.

Svengaard hesitated. The Krebs cycle was following a slow sine curve that dipped perilously into the death cycle now. He knew why Potter had made this decision, but the carcinogenic peril of it had to be weighed. He wondered if he should argue the step. The embryo hung less than four points from a deadly plunge into dissolution. Chemical mutagens administered at this point could shock it into a spurt of growth or destroy it. Even if the mutagen treatment worked, it could leave the embryo susceptible to cancer.

"Mutagen desensitizer!" Potter repeated.

"Dosage?" Svengaard asked.

"Half minim on fractional-minim feed. I'll control it from here."

Svengaard shifted the feeder keys, his eyes on the Krebs-cycle repeater. He'd never heard of applying such drastic treatment this close to the borderline. Mutagens usually were reserved for the partly-flawed Sterrie embryo, a move that sometimes produced dramatic results. It was like shaking a bucket of sand to level the grains. Sometimes the germ plasm presented with a mutagen sought a better level on its own. They'd even produced an occasional viable this way . . . but never an Optiman.

Potter reduced amplification, studied the flow of movement in the embryo. Gently, he depressed the feeder key, searched for Optiman signs. The cellular action remained unsteady, partly blurred.

"Krebs cycle twenty-two eight," the computer nurse said.

Climbing a bit, Potter thought.

"Very slow," Svengaard said.

Potter maintained his vigil within the morula. It was growing, expanding in fits and starts, fighting with all the enormous power contracted in its tiny domain.

"Krebs cycle thirty point four," Svengaard said.

"I am withdrawing mutagens," Potter said. He backed off the microscope to a peripheral cell, desensitized the nucleoproteins, searched for the flawed configurations.

The cell was clean.

Potter traced down into the coiled-coil helices of the DNA chains with a dawning wonder.

"Krebs cycle thirty-six eight and climbing," Svengaard said. "Shall I start the choline and aneurin?"

Potter spoke automatically, his attention fixed on the cell's gene structure. "Yes, start them." He completed the scope tracing, shifted to another peripheral cell.

Identical.

Another cell—the same.

The altered gene pattern held true, but it was a pattern, Potter realized, which hadn't been seen in humankind since the second century of gene shaping. He thought of calling for a comparison to be sure. The computer would have it, of course. No record was ever lost or thrown away. But he dared not . . . there was too much at stake in this. He knew he didn't need the comparison, though. This was a classic form, a classroom norm which he had stared at almost daily all through his medical education.

The super-genius pattern that had caused Sven to call in a Central specialist was there, firmed up by the cutting-room adjustments. It was close-coupled, though, with a fully stable fertility pattern. The longevity basics lay locked in the configurations of the gene structure.

If this embryo reached maturity and encountered a fertile mate, it could breed healthy, living children without the interference of the gene surgeon. It needed no enzyme prescription to survive. It would outlive ten standard humans without that prescription . . . and with a few delicate enzymic adjustments might join the ranks of the immortals.

The Durant embryo could father a new race—like the live-forevers of Central, but dramatically unlike them. This embryo's progeny might fit themselves into the rhythms of natural selectivity . . . completely outside Optiman control.

It was the template pattern from which no human could deviate too far and live, yet it was the single thing feared most by Central.

Every gene surgeon had this drummed into him during his education, *"Natural selectivity is a madness that sends its human victims groping blindly through empty lives."*

Optiman reason and Optiman logic must do the selecting.

As though he straddled Time, Potter felt the profound certainty that the Durant embryo, if it matured, *would* encounter a fertile mate. This embryo had received a gift from *outside*—a wealth of sperm-arginine, the key to its fertility pattern. In the flood of mutagen which opened the active centers of the DNA, this embryo's gene patterns had shaken down into a stable form no human dared attempt.

Why did I introduce the mutagens just then? Potter wondered. *I knew it was the needed thing. How did I know? Was I an instrument of some other force?*

"Krebs cycle fifty-eight and climbing steadily," Svengaard said.

Potter longed for the freedom to discuss this problem with Svengaard . . . but there were the damnable parents and the Security people . . . watching. *Was it possible any-one else had seen enough and knew enough of this pattern to realize what had happened here?* he wondered.

Why did I introduce the mutagens?

"Can you see the pattern yet?" Svengaard asked.

"Not yet," Potter lied.

The embryo was growing rapidly now. Potter studied the proliferation of stable cells. It was beautiful.

"Krebs cycle sixty-four seven," Svengaard said.

I've waited too long, Potter thought. *The bigdomes of Central will ask why I waited so long to kill this embryo. I cannot kill it! It's too beautiful.*

Central maintained its power by keeping the world at large in ignorance of the ruling fist, by doling out living time in the form of precious enzyme prescriptions to its half-alive slaves.

The Folk had a saying: *"In this world there are two worlds—one that works not and lives forever; one that lives not and works forever."*

Here in a crystal vat lay a tiny ball of cells, a living creature less than six-tenths of a millimeter in diameter, and it carried the full potential of living out its life beyond Central's control.

This morula had to die.

They'll order it killed, Potter thought. *And I will be sus-pect . . . finished. And if this thing did get loose in the world, what then? What would happen to gene surgery? Would we go back to correcting minor defects . . . the way it was before we started shaping supermen?*

Supermen!

In his mind, he did what no voice could do: he cursed the Optimen. They were enormous power, instant life or death. Many were geniuses. But they were as dependent on the enzymic fractions as any clod of the Sterries or Breeders. There were men as brilliant among the Sterries and Breeders . . . and among the surgeons.

But none of these could live forever, secure in that ultimate, brutal power.

"Krebs cycle one hundred even," Svengaard said.

"We're over the top now," Potter said. He risked a glance at the computer nurse, but she had her back to him, fussing with her board. Without that computer record, it might be possible to conceal what had happened here. With that record open to examination by Security and by the Optimen, it could not be hidden. Svengaard had not seen enough. The forehead lens only approximated the full field vision. The vat nurses couldn't even guess at it. Only the computer nurse with her tiny monitor screen might know . . . and the full record lay in her machine now—a pattern of magnetic waves on strips of tape.

"That's the lowest I've ever seen it go without killing the embryo," Svengaard said.

"How low?" Potter asked.

"Twenty-one nine," Svengaard said. "Twenty's bottom, of course, but I've never heard of an embryo coming back from below twenty-five before, have you, Doctor?"

"No," Potter said.

"Is it the pattern we want?" Svengaard asked.

"I don't want to interfere too much yet," Potter said.

"Of course," Svengaard said. "Whatever happens, it was inspired surgery."

Inspired surgery! Potter thought. *What would this dolt say if I told him what I have here? A totally viable embryo! A total. Kill it, he'd say. It'll need no enzyme prescription and it can breed true. It hasn't a defect . . . not one. Kill it, he'd say. He's a dutiful slave. The whole sorry history of gene shaping could be justified by this one embryo. But the minute they see this tape at Central, the embryo will be destroyed.*

Eliminate it, they'll say . . . because they don't like to use words too close to kill or death.

Potter bent to the scope. How lovely the embryo was in its own terrifying way.

He risked another glance at the computer nurse. She turned, mask down, met his gaze, smiled. It was a knowing, secretive smile, the smile of a conspirator. Now, she reached up to mop the perspiration from her face. Her sleeve brushed a switch. A rasping, whirring scream came from the computer board. She whirled to it, grated, "Oh, my God!" Her hands sped over the board, but tape continued to hiss through the transponder plates. She turned, tried to wrestle the transparent cover from the recording console. The big reels whirled madly under the cover plate.

"It's running wild!" she shouted.

"It's locked on Erase!" Svengaard yelled. He jumped to her side, tried to get the cover plate off. It jammed in its tracks.

Potter watched like a man in a trance as the last of the tape flashed through the heads, began whipping on the take-up reels.

"Oh, Doctor, we've lost it!" the computer nurse wailed.

Potter focused on the little monitor screen at the computer nurse's station. *Did she watch the operation closely?* he asked himself. *Sometimes they follow the cut move by move ... and computer nurses are a savvy lot. If she watched, she'll have a good idea what we achieved. At the very least, she'll suspect. Was that tape erasure really an accident? Do I dare?*

She turned, met his gaze. "Oh, Doctor, I'm so sorry," she said.

"It's all right, nurse," Potter said. "There's nothing very special about this embryo now, aside from the fact that it will live."

"We missed it, eh?" Svengaard asked. "Must've been the mutagens."

"Yes," Potter said. "But without them it'd have died."

Potter stared at the nurse. He couldn't be sure, but he thought he saw a profound relief wash over her features.

"I'll cut a verbal tape of the operation," Potter said. "That should be enough on this embryo."

And he thought, *When does a conspiracy begin? Was this such a beginning?*

There was still so much this conspiracy required. No knowledgeable eye could ever again look at this embryo through the microscope without being a part of the conspiracy . . . or a traitor.

"We still have the protein synthesis tape," Svengaard said. "That'll give us the chemical factors by reference—and the timing."

Potter thought about the protein synthesis tape. Was there danger in it? No, it was only a reference for what had been used in the operation . . . not *how* anything had been used.

"So it will," Potter said. "So it will." He gestured to the monitor screen. "Operation's finished. You can cut the direct circuit and escort the parents to the reception room. I'm very sorry we achieved no more than we did, but this'll be a healthy human."

"Sterrie?" Svengaard asked.

"Too soon to guess," Potter said. He looked at the computer nurse. She had managed to get the cover off at last and had stopped the tapes. "Any idea how that happened?"

"Probably solonoid failure," Svengaard said.

"This equipment's quite old," the nurse said. "I've asked for replacement units several times, but we don't seem to be very high on the priority lists."

And there's a natural reluctance at Central to admit anything can wear out, Potter thought.

"Yes," Potter said. "Well, I daresay you'll get your replacements now."

Did anyone else see her trip that switch? Potter wondered. He tried to remember where everyone in the room had been looking, worried that a Security monitor might've been watching her. *If Security saw that, she's dead*, Potter thought. *And so am I.*

"The technician's report on repairs will have to be part of the record on this case," Svengaard said. "I presume you'll—"

"I'll see to it personally, Doctor," she said.

Turning away, Potter had the impression that he and the computer nurse had just carried on a silent conversation. He noted that the big screen was now a gray blank, the

Durants no longer watching. *Should I see them myself?* he wondered. *If they're part of the Underground, they could help. Something has to be done about the embryo. Safest to get it out of here entirely . . . but how?*

"I'll take care of the tie-off details," Svengaard said. He began checking the vat seals, life systems repeaters, dismantling the meson generator.

Someone has to see the parents, Potter thought.

"The parents'll be disappointed," Svengaard said. "They generally know why a specialist is called in . . . and probably got their hopes up."

The door from the ready room opened to admit a man Potter recognized as an agent from Central Security. He was a moon-faced blond with features one tended to forget five minutes after leaving him. The man crossed the room to stand in front of Potter.

Is this the end for me? Potter wondered. He forced his voice into a steady casual tone, asked, "What about the parents?"

"They're clean," the agent said. "No tricky devices—conversation normal . . . plenty of small talk, but normal."

"No hint of the other things?" Potter asked. "Any way they could've penetrated Security without instruments?"

"Impossible!" the man snorted.

"Doctor Svengaard believes the father's overly endowed with male protectiveness and the mother has too much maternalism," Potter said.

"The records show you shaped 'em," the agent said.

"It's possible," Potter said. "Sometimes you have to concentrate on gross elements of the cut to save the embryo. Little things slip past."

"Anything slip past on this one today?" the agent asked. "I understand the tape's been erased . . . an accident."

Does he suspect? Potter asked himself. The extent of his own involvement and personal danger threatened to overwhelm Potter. It took the greatest effort to maintain a casual tone.

"Anything's possible of course," Potter said. He shrugged. "But I don't think we have anything unusual here. We lost the Optishape in saving the embryo, but that happens. We can't win them all."

"Should we flag the embryo's record?" the agent asked.

He's still fishing, Potter told himself. He said, "Suit yourself. I'll have a verbal tape on the cut pretty soon—probably just as accurate as the visual one. You might wait and analyze that before you decide."

"I'll do that," the agent said.

Svengaard had the microscope off the vat now. Potter relaxed slightly. No one was going to take a casual, dangerous look at the embryo.

"I guess we brought you on a wild goose chase," Potter said. "Sorry about that, but they did insist on watching."

"Better ten wild goose chases than one set of parents knowing too much," the agent said. "How was the tape erased?"

"Accident," Potter said. "Worn equipment. We'll have the technical report for you shortly."

"Leave the worn equipment thing out of your report," the agent said. "I'll take that verbally. Allgood has to show every report to the Tuyere now."

Potter permitted himself an understanding nod. "Of course." The men who worked out of Central knew about such things. One concealed personally disquieting items from the Optimen.

The agent glanced around the cutting room, said, "Someday we won't have to use all this secrecy. Won't come any too soon for me." He turned away.

Potter watched the retreating back, thinking how neatly the agent fitted into the demands of his profession. A superb cut with just one flaw—too neat a fit, too much cold logic, not enough imaginative curiosity and readiness to explore the avenues of chance.

If he'd pressed me, he'd have had me, Potter thought. *He should've been more curious about the accident. But we tend to copy our masters—even in their blind spots.*

Potter began to have more confidence of success in his impetuous venture. He turned back to help Svengaard with the final details, wondering, *How do I know the agent's satisfied with my explanation.* No feeling of disquiet accompanied the question. *I know he's satisfied, but how do I know it?* Potter asked himself.

He realized then that his mind had been absorbing correlated gene information—the inner workings of the cells and their exterior manifestations—for so many years that this weight of data had fused into a new level of understanding. He was reading the tiny betrayals in gene-type reactions.

I can read people!

It was a staggering realization. He looked around the room at the nurses helping with the tie-off. When his eyes found the computer nurse, he *knew* she had deliberately destroyed the record tape. He knew it.

4

Lizbeth and Harvey Durant walked hand in hand from the hospital after their interview with the Doctors Potter and Svengaard. They smiled and swung their clasped hands like children off on a picnic—which in a sense they were.

The morning's rain had been shut off and the clouds were being packed off to the east, toward the tall peaks that looked down on Seatac Megalopolis. The overhead sky showed a clear cerulean blue with a goblin sun riding high in it.

A mob of people in loose marching order was coming through the park across the way, obviously the exercise period for some factory team or labor group. Their uniformed sameness was broken by flashes of color—an orange scarf on a woman's head, a yellow sash across a man's chest, the scarlet of a fertility fetish dangling on a gold loop from a woman's ear. One man had equipped himself bright green shoes.

The pathetic attempts at individuality in a world of gene-stamped sameness stabbed through Lizbeth's defenses. She turned away lest the scene tear the smile from her lips, asked, "Where'll we go?"

"Hmmm?" Harvey held her back, waiting on the walk for the group to pass.

Among the marchers, faces turned to stare enviously at Harvey and Lizbeth. All knew why the Durants were here. The hospital, a great pile of plasmeld behind them, the fact that they were man and woman together, the casual dress, the smiles—all said the Durants were on breeder-leave from their appointed labors.

Each individual in that mob hoped with a lost desperation for this same escape from the routine that bound them all. Viable gametes, breeder leave—it was the universal dream. Even the known Sterries hoped, and patronized the breeder quacks and the manufacturers of doombah fetishes.

They have no pasts, Lizbeth thought, focusing abruptly on the common observation of the Folk philosophers. *They're all people without pasts and only the hope for a future to cling to. Somewhere our past was lost in an ocean of darkness. The Optimen and their gene surgeons have extinguished our past.*

Even their own breeder-leave lost its special glow in the face of this. The Durants might not be constrained to leap up at the rising bell and hurry apart to their labors, but they were still people without a past . . . and their future might be lost in an instant. The child being formed in the hospital vat . . . in some small way it might still be part of them, but the surgeons had changed it. They had cut it off sharply from its past.

Lizbeth recalled her own parents, the feeling of estrangement from them, of differences which went deeper than blood.

They were only partly my parents, she thought. *They knew it . . . and I knew it.*

She felt the beginnings of estrangement from her own unformed son then, an emotion that colored present necessities. *What's the use?* she wondered. But she knew what the use was—to end forever all this amputation of pasts.

The last envious face passed. The mob became moving backs, bits of color. They turned a corner and were gone, cut off.

Is it a corner we've turned and no coming back? Lizbeth wondered.

"Let's walk to the cross-town shuttle tube," Harvey said.

"Through the park?" she asked.

"Yes," Harvey said. "Just think—ten months."

"And we can take our son home," she said. "We're very lucky."

"It seems like a long time—ten months," Harvey said.

Lizbeth answered as they crossed the street and entered the park. "Yes, but we can come see him every week when they shift him to the big vat—and that's only three months away."

"You're right," Harvey said. "It'll be over before we know it. And thank the powers he's not a specialist or *anything else*. We can raise him at home. Our work time'll be reduced."

"That Doctor Potter's wonderful," she said.

As they talked, their clasped hands moved with the subtle pressures and finger shifts of the secret conversation—the *No-Spoken-Word* hand code that classified them as couriers of the Parents Underground.

"They're still watching us," Harvey signaled.

"I know."

"Svengaard is out—a slave of the power structure."

"Obviously. You know, I had no idea the computer nurse was one of us."

"You saw that, too?"

"Potter was looking at her when she tripped the switch."

"Do you think the Security people saw her?"

"Not a chance. They were all concentrated on us."

"Maybe she's not one of us," Harvey signaled. And he spoke aloud, "Isn't it a beautiful day. Let's take the floral path."

Lizbeth's finger pressures answered, *"You think that nurse is an accidental?"*

"Could be. Perhaps she saw what Potter'd accomplished and knew there was only one way to save the embryo."

"Someone will have to contact her immediately then."

"*Cautiously. She might be unstable, emotional—a breeder neurotic.*"

"*What about Potter?*"

"*We'll have to get people to him right away. We'll need his help getting the embryo out of there.*"

"*That'll give us nine of Central's surgeons,*" she said.

"*If he goes along,*" Harvey signaled.

She looked at him with a smile that completely masked her sudden worry. "*You have doubts?*"

"*It's only that I think he was reading me at the same time I read him.*"

"*Oh, he was,*" she said. "*But he was slow and lame about it compared to us.*"

"*That's how I read him. He was like a first reader, an amateur stumbling along, gaining confidence as he went.*"

"*He's untrained,*" she said. "*That's obvious. I was worried you'd read something in him that escaped me.*"

"*I guess you're right.*"

Across the park, dust had shattered the sunlight into countless pillars that stood up through an arboretum. Lizabeth stared at the scene as she answered, "*No doubt of it, darling. He's a natural, someone who's stumbled onto the talent accidentally. They do occur, you know—have to. Nothing can keep us from communicating.*"

"*But they certainly try.*"

"*Yes,*" she signaled. "*They were very intent on it there today, probing and scanning us in that lounge. But people who think mechanically will never guess—I mean that our weapons are people and not things.*"

"*It's their fatal blind spot,*" he agreed. "*Central's carved out the genetic ruts with logic—and logic keeps digging the ruts deeper and deeper. They're so deep now they can't see over the edges to the outside.*"

"*And that wide, wide universe out there calling to us,*" she signaled.

5

Max Allgood, Central's chief of Tachy-Security, climbed Administration's plasmeld steps slightly ahead of his two surgeon companions as befitted the director of the Optimen's swift and terrible hand of power.

The morning sun behind the trio sent their shadows darting across the white building's angles and planes.

They were admitted to the silver shadows of the entrance portico where a barrier dropped for the inevitable delay. Quarantine scanners searched and probed them for inimical microbes.

Allgood turned with the patience of long experience in this procedure, studied his companions—Boumour and Igan. It amused him that they must drop their titles here. No doctors were admitted to these precincts. Here they must be pharmacists. The title "doctor" carried overtones which spread unrest among the Optimen. *They* knew about doctors, but only as ministers to the *mere* humans. A doctor became a euphemism in here, just as no one said *death* or *kill* or implied that a machine or structure would wear out. Only new Optimen in their acolyte apprenticeship, or *meres* of young appearance served in Central, although some of the *meres* had been preserved by their masters for remarkable lengths of time.

Boumour and Inga both passed the test of youthfulness, although Boumour's face was of that pinched-up elfin type which tended to suggest age before its time. He was a big man with heavy shoulders, powerful. Igan looked lean and fragile beside him, a beaked face with long jaw and tight little mouth. The eyes of both men were Optimen color—blue and penetrating. They were probably near-Opts, both of them. Most Central surgeon-pharmacists were.

The pair moved restlessly under Allgood's gaze, avoiding his eyes. Boumour began talking in a low voice to Igan with one hand on the man's shoulder moving nervously, kneading. The movement of Boumour's hand on Igan's shoulder carried an odd familiarity, a suggestion to Allgood that he had seen something like this somewhere before. He couldn't place where.

The quarantine probing-scanning continued. It seemed to Allgood that it was lasting longer than usual. He turned his attention to the scene across from the building. It was strangely peaceful, at odds with the mood of Central as Allgood knew it.

Allgood realized that his access to secret records and even to old books gave him an uncommon knowledge about Central. The Optiman demesne reached across leagues of what had once been the political entities of Canada and northern United States. It occupied a rough circle some seven hundred kilometers in diameter and with two hundred levels below ground. It was a region of multitudinous controls—weather control, gene control, bacterial control, enzyme control . . . human control . . .

In this little corner, the heart of Administration, the ground had been shaped into an Italian chiaroscuro landscape—blacks and grays with touches of pastels. The Optimen were people who could barber a mountain at a whim: *"A little off the top and leave the sideburns."* Throughout Central, nature had been smoothed over, robbed of her dangerous sharpness. Even when the Optimen staged some natural display, it lacked an element of drama which was a general lack in their lives.

Allgood often wondered at this. He had seen pre-

Optiman films and recognized the differences. Central's manicured niceties seemed to him all tied up with the omnipresent red triangles indicating pharmacy outlets where the Optimen might check their enzyme prescriptions.

"Are they taking a long time about it or is it just me?" Boumour asked. His voice carried a rumbling quality.

"Patience," Igan said. A mellow tenor there.

"Yes," Allgood said. "Patience is a man's best ally."

Boumour looked up at the Security chief, studying, wondering. Allgood seldom spoke except for effect. He, not the Optimen, was the Conspiracy's greatest threat. He was body and soul with his masters, a super puppet. *Why did he order us to accompany him today?* Boumour wondered. *Does he know? Will he denounce us?*

There was a special ugliness about Allgood that fascinated Boumour. The Security chief was a stocky little Folk *mere* with moon face and darting almond eyes, a dark bush of hair low on his forehead—a Shang-cut by the look of his overt gene markers.

Allgood turned toward the quarantine barrier and with a sudden feeling of awakening, Boumour realized the man's ugliness came from within. It was the ugliness of fear, of created fear and personal fear. The realization gave Boumour an abrupt sensation of relief which he signaled to Igan through finger pressures on the man's shoulder.

Igan pulled away suddenly to stare out across from the building where they stood. *Of course Max Allgood fears,* he thought. *He lives in a mire of fears, named and nameless . . . just as the Optimen do . . . poor creatures.*

The scene across from Central began to impress itself on Igan's senses. Here, at this moment, it was a day of absolute Spring, planned that way in the lordly heart of Weather Control. Administration's steps looked down on a lake, round and perfect like an enameled blue plate. On a low hill beyond the lake, plasmeld plinths stood out like white stones: elevator caps reaching down into the locked fastness of the Optimen quarters below—two hundred levels.

Far beyond the hill, the sky began to turn dark blue and oily. It was streaked suddenly with red, green and purple

fires in a rather flat pattern. Presently, there came a low
clap of contained thunder. Across the reaches of Central,
some Upper Optiman was staging a tame storm for entertainment.

It struck Igan as a pointless display, lacking danger or
drama . . . which he decided were two words for the same
thing.

The storm was the first thing Allgood had seen this day
to fit his interpretation of Central's inner rhythms. Things
of an ominous nature set the pattern for his view of Central.
People vanished into here never to be seen again and only
he, Allgood, the chief of Tachy-Security, or a few trusted
agents knew their fate. Allgood felt the thunderclap keyed
to his mood, a sound that portended absolute power. Under
the storm sky now turning acid yellow and dispersing the
air of Spring, the plinths on the hill above the lake became
pagan cenotaphs set out against a ground as purple-green
as camomile.

"It's time," Boumour said.

Allgood turned to find the quarantine barrier lifted. He
led the way into the Hall of Counsel with its shimmering
adamantine walls above ranks of empty plasmeld benches.
The trio moved through tongues of perfumed vapor that
swayed aside as they breasted them.

Optiman acolytes wearing green capes fastened at the
shoulders with diamond lanulas came from side shadows
to pace them. Worked into the green of their robes were
shepherd's pipes of platinum and they swung golden thuribles that wafted clouds of antiseptic pink smoke into the
air.

Allgood kept his attention on the end of the hall. A giant
globe as red as a mandrake stem hung in walking beams
there. It was some forty meters in diameter with a section
folded back like a segment cut from an orange to reveal
the interior. This was the Tuyere's control center, the tool
of strange powers and senses with which *they* watched and
ruled their minions. Lights flashed in there, phosphor
greens and the blue cracklings of arcs. Great round gauges
spelled out messages and red lights winked response. Num-

bers flowed on beams through the air and esoteric symbols danced on ribbons of light.

Up through the middle, like the core of the fruit, stretched a white column supporting a triangular platform at the globe's center. At the points of the triangle, each on a golden plasmeld throne, sat the Optimen trio known as the Tuyere—friends, companions, elected rulers for this century and with seventy-eight years yet to serve. It was a wink of time in their lives, an annoyance, often disquieting because they must face realities which all other Optimen could treat as euphemisms.

The acolytes stopped some twenty paces from the red globe, but continued swinging their thuribles. Allgood moved one pace ahead, motioned Boumour and Igan to halt behind him. The Security chief felt he knew just how far he could go here, that he must go to the limits. *They need me*, he told himself. But he held no illusions about the dangers in this interview.

Allgood looked up into the globe. A dancing lacery of power placed a deceptive transparency over the interior. Through that curtain could be seen shapes, outlines—now clear, now enfolded.

"I came," Allgood said.

Boumour and Igan echoed the greeting, reminding themselves of all the protocol and forms which must be observed here: *"Always use the name of the Optiman you address. If you do not know the name, ask it humbly."*

Allgood waited for the Tuyere to answer. Sometimes he felt they had no sense of time, at least of seconds and minutes and perhaps not even of days. It might be true. People of infinite lives might notice the passing seasons as clock ticks.

The throne support turned, presenting the Tuyere one by one. They sat in clinging translucent robes, almost nude, flaunting their similarity to the *meres*. Facing the open segment now was Nourse, a Greek god figure with blocky face, heavy brows, a chest ridged by muscles that rippled as he breathed. How evenly he breathed, with what controlled slowness.

The base turned, presented Schruille, the bone slender, unpredictable one with great round eyes, high cheeks and a flat nose above a mouth which seemed always pulled into a thin line of disapproval. Here was a dangerous one. Some said he spoke of things which other Optimen could not. In Allgood's presence, Schruille had once said "death," although referring to a butterfly.

Again, the base turned—and here was Calapine, her robe girdled with crystal plastrons. She was a thin, high-breasted woman with golden brown hair and chill, insolent eyes, full lips and a long nose above a pointed chin. Allgood had caught her watching him strangely on occasion. At such times he tried not to think about the Optimen who took *mere* playmates.

Nourse spoke to Calapine, looking at her through the prismatic reflector which each throne raised at a shoulder. She answered, but the voices did not carry to the floor of the hall.

Allgood watched the interplay for a clue to their mood. It was known among the Folk that Nourse and Calapine had been bedmates for periods that spanned hundreds of *mere* lifetimes. Nourse had a reputation of strength and predictability, but Calapine was known as a wild one. Mention her name and likely someone would look up and ask, "What's she done now?" It was always said with a touch of admiration and fear. Allgood knew that fear. He had worked for other ruling trios, but none who had his measure as did these three . . . especially Calapine.

The throne base stopped with Nourse facing the open segment. "You came," he rumbled. "Of course you came. The ox knows its owner and the ass its master's crib."

So it's going to be one of those days, Allgood thought. *Ridicule!* It could only mean they knew how he had stumbled . . . but didn't they always?

Calapine swiveled her throne to look down at the *meres.* The Hall of Counsel had been patterned on the Roman Senate with false columns around the edges, banks of benches beneath glittering scanner eyes. Everything focused down onto the figures standing apart from the acolytes.

Looking up, Igan reminded himself he had feared and hated these creatures all his life—even while he pitied them. How lucky he'd been to miss the Optiman cut. It'd been close, but he'd been saved. He could remember the hate of his childhood, before it had become tempered by pity. It'd been a clean thing then, sharp and real, blazing against the Givers of Time.

"We came as requested to report on the Durants," Allgood said. He took two deep breaths to calm his nerves. These sessions were always dangerous, but doubly so since he'd decided on a double game. There was no turning back, though, and no wish to since he'd discovered the dopplegangers of himself they were growing. There could be only one reason they'd duplicate him. Well, they'd learn.

Calapine studied Allgood, wondering if it might be time to seek diversion with the ugly Folk male. Perhaps here was an answer to boredom. Both Schruille and Nourse indulged. She seemed to recall having done that before with another Max, but couldn't remember if it had helped her boredom.

"Say what it is we give you, little Max," she said.

Her woman's voice, soft and with laughter behind it, terrified him. Allgood swallowed. "You give life, Calapine."

"Say how many lovely years you have," she ordered.

Allgood found his throat contained no moisture. "Almost four hundred, Calapine," he rasped.

Nourse chuckled. "Ahead of you stretch many more lovely years if you serve us well," he said.

It was the closest to a direct threat Allgood had ever heard from an Optiman. They worked their wills by indirection, by euphemistic subtlety. They worked through *meres* who could face such concepts as death and killing.

Who have they shaped to destroy me? Allgood wondered.

"Many little tick-tock years," Calapine said.

"Enough!" Schruille growled. He detested these interviews with the underclasses, the way Calapine baited the Folk. He swiveled his throne and now all the Tuyere faced the open segment. Schruille looked at his fingers, the ever youthful skin, and wondered why he had snapped that way. An enzymic imbalance? The thought touched him with disquiet. He generally held his silence during these sessions— as a defense because he tended to get sentimental about the pitiful *meres* and despise himself for it afterward.

Boumour moved up beside Allgood, said, "Does the Tuyere wish now the report on the Durants?"

Allgood stifled a feeling of rage at the interruption. Didn't the fool know that the Optimen must always appear to lead the interview?

"The words and images of your report have been seen, analyzed and put away," Nourse rumbled. "Now, it is the non-report that we wish."

Non-report? Allgood asked himself. *Does he think we've hidden something?*

"Little Max," Calapine said. "Have you bowed to our necessity and questioned the computer nurse under narcosis?"

Here it comes, Allgood thought. He took a deep breath, said, "She has been questioned, Calapine."

Igan took his place beside Boumour, said, "There's something I wish to say about that if I—"

"Hold your tongue, pharmacist," Nourse said. "We talk to Max."

Igan bowed his head, thought, *How dangerous this is! And all because of that fool nurse. She wasn't even one of us. No Cyborg-of-the-register knows her. A member of no cell or platoon. An accidental, a Sterrie, and she puts us in this terrible peril!*

Allgood saw that Igan's hands trembled, wondered, *What's driving these surgeons? They can't be such fools.*

"Was it not a deliberate thing that nurse did?" Calapine asked.

"Yes, Calapine," Allgood said.

"Your agents did not see it, yet we knew it had to be," Calapine said. She turned to scan the instruments of the control center, returned her attention to Allgood. "Say now why this was."

Allgood sighed. "I have no excuses, Calapine. The men have been censured."

"Say now why the nurse acted thus," Calapine ordered.

Allgood wet his lips with his tongue, glanced at Boumour and Igan. They looked at the floor. He looked back to Calapine, at her face shimmering within the globe. "We were unable to discover her motives, Calapine."

"Unable?" Nourse demanded.

"She . . . ahh . . . ceased to exist during the interrogation, Nourse," Allgood said. As the Tuyere stiffened, sitting bolt upright in their thrones, he added, "A flaw in her genetic cutting, so the pharmacists tell me."

"A profound pity," Nourse said, settling back.

Igan looked up, blurted, "It could've been a deliberate self-erasure, Nourse."

That damn' fool! Allgood thought.

But Nourse stared now at Igan. "You were present, Igan?"

"Boumour and I administered the narcotics."

And she died, Igan thought. *But we did not kill her. She died and we'll be blamed for it. Where could she have learned the trick of stopping her own heart? Only Cyborgs are supposed to know and teach it.*

"Deliberate . . . self-erasure?" Nourse asked. Even when considered indirectly, the idea held terrifying implications.

"Max!" Calapine said. "Say now if you used excessive . . . cruelty." She leaned forward, wondering why she wanted him to admit barbarity.

"She suffered nothing, Calapine;" Allgood said.

Calapine sat back disappointed. *Could he be lying?* She read her instruments: Calmness. He wasn't lying.

"Pharmacist," Nourse said, "explain your opinion."

"We examined her carefully," Igan said. "It couldn't have been the narcotics. There's no way . . ."

"Some of us think it was a genetic flaw," Boumour said.

"There's disagreement," Igan said. He glanced at Allgood, feeling the man's disapproval. It had to be done, though. The Optimen must be made to know disquiet. When they could be tricked into acting emotionally, they made mistakes. The plan called for them to make mistakes now. They must be put off balance—subtly, delicately.

"Your opinion, Max?" Nourse asked. He watched carefully. They'd been getting poorer models lately, doppleganger degeneration.

"We've already taken cellular matter, Nourse," Allgood said, "and are growing a duplicate. If we get a true copy, we'll check the question of genetic flaw."

"It is a pity the doppleganger won't have the original's memories," Nourse said.

"Pity of pities," Calapine said. She looked at Schruille "Is this not true, Schruille?"

Schruille looked up at her without answering. Did she think she could bait him the way she did the *meres?*

"This woman had a mate?" Nourse asked.

"Yes, Nourse," Allgood said.

"Fertile union?"

"No, Nourse," Allgood said. "A Sterrie."

"Compensate the mate," Nourse said. "Another woman, a bit of leisure. Let him think she was loyal to us."

Allgood nodded, said, "We are giving him a woman, Nourse, who will keep him under constant surveillance."

A trill of laughter escaped Calapine. "Why has no one mentioned this Potter, the genetic engineer?" she asked.

"I was coming to him, Calapine," Allgood said.

"Has anyone examined the embryo?" Schruille asked, looking up suddenly.

"No, Schruille," Allgood said.

"Why not?"

"If this is a concerted action to escape genetic controls, Schruille, we don't want members of the organization to know we suspect them. Not yet. First, we must learn all about these people—the Durants, their friends, Potter . . . everyone."

"But the embryo's the key to the entire thing," Schruille said. "What was done to it? What is it?"

"It is bait, Schruille," Allgood said. "Bait?"

"Yes, Schruille, to catch whoever else may be involved."

"But what was done to it?"

"How can that matter, Schruille, as long as we can . . . as long as we have complete control over it."

"The embryo is being guarded most adroitly, I hope," Nourse said.

"Most adroitly, Nourse."

"Send the pharmacist Svengaard to us," Calapine ordered.

"Svengaard . . . Calapine?" Allgood asked.

"You need not know why," she said. "Merely send him."

"Yes, Calapine."

She stood up to signify the end of the interview. The acolytes turned around, still swinging their thuribles, prepared now to escort the *meres* from the hall. But Calapine was not finished. She stared at Allgood, said, "Look at me, Max."

He looked, recognizing that strange, studying set to her eyes.

"Am I not beautiful?" she asked.

Allgood stared at her, the slender figure with its outlines softened by the robe and curtains of power within the globe. She was beautiful as were many Optimen females. But the beauty repelled him with its threatening perfection. She would live indefinitely, already had lived forty or fifty thousand years. But one day his lesser flesh would reject the medical replacements and the enzyme prescriptions. He would die while she went on and on and on.

His lesser flesh rejected her.

"You are beautiful, Calapine," he said.

"Your eyes never admit it," she said.

"What do you want, Cal?" Nourse asked. "Do you want this . . . do you want Max?"

"I want his eyes," she said. "Just his eyes."

Nourse looked at Allgood, said, "Women." His voice held a note of false camaraderie.

Allgood stood astonished. He had never heard that tone from an Optiman before.

"I make a point," Calapine said. "Don't interrupt my words with male jokes. In your heart of hearts, Max, how do you feel about me?"

"Ahhhh," Nourse said. He nodded.

"I shall say it for you," she said as Allgood remained mute. "You worship me. Never forget that, Max. You worship me." She looked at Boumour and Igan, dismissed them with a wave of her hand.

Allgood lowered his eyes, feeling the truth in her words. He turned, and with the acolytes flanking them, led Igan and Boumour out of the hall.

As they emerged onto the steps, the acolytes held back and the barrier dropped. Igan and Boumour turned left, noting a new building at the end of the long esplanade which fronted Administration. They saw its machicolated walls, the openings fitted with colored filters which sent bursts of red, blue and green light upon the surrounding air, and they recognized that it blocked the way they had intended to take out of Central. A building suddenly erected, another Optiman toy. They saw it and planned their steps accordingly with the automatic acceptance that marked them as regulars in the Optiman demesne. The *meres* and inhabitants of Central seemed to know their way through the arabesques of its roads and streets by an instinct. The place defied cartographers because the Optimen were too subject to change and whim.

"Igan!"

It was Allgood calling from behind them.

They turned, waited for him to catch up.

Allgood planted himself in front of them, hands on hips, said, "Do you worship her, too?"

"Don't speak foolishness," Boumour said.

"No," Allgood said. His eyes appeared to be sunk in pockets above the high cheekbones. "I belong to no Folk cult, no breeder congregation. How can I worship her?"

"But you do," Igan said.

"Yes!"

"They are the real religion of our world," Igan said. "You do not have to belong to a cult or carry a talisman to know this. Calapine merely told you that, if there is a conspiracy, those belonging to it are heretics."

"Is that what she meant?"

"Of course."

"And she must know what is done to heretics," Allgood said.

"Without a doubt," Boumour said.

6

Svengaard had seen this building in the tri-casts and entertainment vids. He'd heard descriptions of the Hall of Counsel—but actually to be standing here at the quarantine wall with the copper sheen of sunset over the hills across from it . . . he'd never dreamed this could occur.

Elevator caps stood out like plasmeld warts on the hillock in front of him. There were other low hills beyond with piled buildings on them that could've been mistaken for rock outcroppings.

A lone woman passed him on the esplanade pulling a ground-effect cart filled with oddly shaped bundles. Svengaard found himself worried about what the bundles might contain, but he knew he dared not ask or show undue curiosity.

The red triangle of a pharmacy outlet glowed on a pillar beside him. He passed it, glanced back at his escort.

He had come halfway across the continent in the tube with an entire car to himself except for the escort, an agent from T-Security. Deep into Central they'd come, the gray-suited T-Security agent always beside him.

Svengaard began climbing the steps.

Already, Central was beginning to weigh on him. There was a sense of something disastrous about the place. Even though he suspected the source of the feeling, he couldn't shake it off. It was all the Folk nonsense you could never quite evade, he'd decided. The Folk were a people for the most part without legends or ancient myths except where such matters touched the Optimen. In the Folk memories, Central and the Optimen were fixed with sinister omens compounded of awesome fear and adulation.

Why did they summon me? Svengaard asked himself. The escort refused to say.

They were stopped by the wall and waited now, silent, nervous.

Even the agent was nervous, Svengaard saw.

Why did they summon me?

The agent cleared his throat, said, "You have all the protocol straight?"

"I think so," Svengaard said.

"Once you get into the hall, keep pace with the acolytes who'll escort you from there. You'll be interviewed by the Tuyere—Nourse, Schruille and Calapine. Remember to use their names when you address them individually. Use no such words as death or kill or die. Avoid the very concepts if you can. Let them lead the interview. Best not to volunteer anything."

Svengaard took a trembling breath.

Have they brought me here to advance me? he wondered. *That must be it. I've served my apprenticeship under such men as Potter and Igan. I'm being promoted to Central.*

"And don't say 'doctor,' " the escort said. "Doctors are pharmacists or genetic engineers in here."

"I understand," Svengaard said.

"Allgood wants a complete report on the interview afterward," the agent said.

"Yes, of course," Svengaard said.

The quarantine barrier lifted.

"In you go," the agent said.

"You're not coming with me?" Svengaard asked.

"Not invited," the agent said. He turned, went down the steps.

Svengaard swallowed, entered the silver gloom of the

portico, stepped through to find himself in the long hall
with an escort of six acolytes, three to a side, swinging
thuribles from which pink smoke wafted. He smelled the
antiseptics in the smoke.

The big red globe at the end of the hall dominated the
place. Its open segment showing flashing and winking
lights; the moving shapes inside fascinated Svengaard.

The acolytes stopped him twenty paces from the opening
and he looked up at the Tuyere, recognizing them through
the power curtains—Nourse in the center flanked by Calapine and Schruille.

"I came," Svengaard said, mouthing the greeting the
agent had told him to use. He rubbed sweaty palms against
his best tunic.

Nourse spoke with a rumbling voice, "You are the genetic engineer, Svengaard."

"Thei Svengaard, yes . . . Nourse." He took a deep
breath, wondering if they'd caught the hesitation while he
remembered to use the Optiman's name.

Nourse smiled.

"You assisted recently in the genetic alteration of an embryo from a couple named Durant," Nourse said. "The chief
engineer at the cutting was Potter."

"Yes, I was the assistant, Nourse."

"There was an accident during this operation," Calapine
said.

There was a strange musical quality in her voice, and
Svengaard recognized she hadn't asked a question, but had
reminded him of a detail to which she wanted him to give
his attention. He felt the beginnings of a profound disquiet.

"An accident, yes . . . Calapine," he said.

"You followed the operation closely?" Nourse asked.

"Yes, Nourse." And Svengaard found his attention
swinging to Schruille, who sat there brooding and silent.

"Now then," Calapine said, "you will be able to tell us
what it is Potter has concealed about this genetic alteration."

Svengaard found that he had lost his voice. He could
only shake his head.

"He concealed nothing?" Nourse asked. "Is that what you say?"

Svengaard nodded.

"We mean you no harm, Thei Svengaard," Calapine said. "You may speak."

Svengaard swallowed, cleared his throat. "I . . ." he said. ". . . the question . . . I saw nothing . . . concealed." He fell silent, then remembered he was supposed to use her name and said, "Calapine," just as Nourse started to speak.

Nourse broke off, scowled.

Calapine giggled.

Nourse said, "Yet you tell us you followed the genetic alteration."

"I . . . wasn't on the microscope with him every second," Svengaard said. "Nourse. I . . . uh . . . the duties of the assistant—instructions to the computer nurse, keying the feeder tapes and so on."

"Say now if the computer nurse was a special friend of yours," Calapine ordered.

"I . . . she'd . . ." Svengaard wet his lips with his tongue. *What do they want?* "We'd worked together for a number of years, Calapine. I can't say she was a friend. We worked together."

"Did you examine the embryo after the operation?" Nourse asked.

Schruille sat up, stared at Svengaard.

"No, Nourse," Svengaard said. "My duties were to secure the vat, check life support systems." He took a deep breath. Perhaps they were only testing him after all . . . but such odd questions!

"Say now if Potter is a special friend," Calapine ordered.

"He was one of my teachers, Calapine, someone I've worked with on delicate gentic problems."

"But not in your particular circle," Nourse said.

Svengaard shook his head. Again, he sensed menace. He didn't know what to expect—perhaps that the great globe would roll over, crush him, reduce his body to scattered atoms. But no, the Optimen couldn't do that. He studied the three faces as they became clear through the power curtains, seeking a sign. Clean, sterile faces. He could see the genetic markers in their features—they might be any Sterries of the Folk except for the Optiman aura of mystery. Folk rumor said they were sterile by choice, that they saw breeding as the beginning of death, but the genetic clues of their features spoke otherwise to Svengaard.

"Why did you call Potter on this particular problem?" Nourse asked.

Svengaard took a tight, quavering breath, said, "He . . . the embryo's genetic configuration . . . near-Opt. Potter is familiar with our hospital. He . . . I have confidence in him; brilliant sur—genetic engineer."

"Say now if you are friendly with any other of our pharmacists," Calapine said.

"They . . . I work with them when they come to our facility," Svengaard said.

"Calapine," Nourse supplied.

A trill of laughter shook her.

A dark flush spread up from Svengaard's collar. He began to feel angry. What kind of test was this? Couldn't they do anything but sit there, mocking, questioning?

Anger gave Svengaard command of his voice and he said, "I'm only head of genetic engineering at one facility, Nourse—a lowly district engineer. I handle routine cuttings. When something requires a specialist, I follow orders, call a specialist. Potter was the indicated specialist for this case."

"*One* of the specialists," Nourse said.

"One I know and respect," Svengaard said. He didn't bother adding the Optiman's name.

"Say now if you are angry," Calapine ordered, and there was that musical quality in her voice.

"I'm angry."

"Say why."

"Why am I here?" Svengaard asked. "What kind of interrogation is this? Have I done something wrong? Am I to be censured?"

Nourse bent forward, hands on knees. "You dare question us?"

Svengaard stared at the Optiman. In spite of the tone of the question, the square, heavy-boned face appeared reassuring, calming. "I'll do anything I can to help you," Svengaard said. "Anything. But how can I help or answer you when I don't know what you want?"

Calapine started to speak, but stopped as Nourse raised a hand.

"Our most profound wish is that we could tell you," Nourse said. "But surely you know we can have no true discourse. How could you understand what we understand? Can a wooden bowl contain sulphuric acid? Trust us. We seek what is best for you."

A sense of warmth and gratitude permeated Svengaard. Of course he trusted them. They were the genetic apex of humankind. And he reminded himself: *"They are the power that loves us and cares for us."*

Svengaard sighed. "What do you wish of me?"

"You have answered all our questions," Nourse said. "Even our non-questions are answered."

"Now, you will forget everything that has happened here between us," Calapine said. "You will repeat our conversation to no person."

Svengaard cleared his throat. "To no one . . . Calapine?"

"No one."

"Max Allgood has asked that I report to him on—"

"Max must be denied," she said. "Fear not, Thei Svengaard. We will protect you."

"As you command," Svengaard said. "Calapine."

"It is not our wish that you think us ungrateful of your loyalty and services," Nourse said. "We are mindful of your good opinion and would not appear cold nor callous in your eyes. Know that our concern is for the larger good of humankind."

"Yes, Nourse," Svengaard said.

It was a gratuitous speech, its tone disturbing to Svengaard, but it helped clear his reason. He began to see the direction of their curiosity, to sense their suspicions. Those were his suspicions now. Potter had betrayed his trust, had he? The business with the accidentally destroyed tape had not been an accident. Very well—the criminals would pay.

"You may go now," Nourse said.

"With our blessing," Calapine said.

Svengaard bowed. And he marked that Schruille had not spoken or moved during the entire interview. Svengaard wondered why this fact, of itself, should be a suddenly terrifying thing. His knees trembled as he turned, the acolytes flanking him with their smoking thuribles, and left the hall.

The Tuyere watched until the barrier dropped behind Svengaard.

"Another one who doesn't know what Potter achieved." Calapine said.

"Are you sure Max doesn't know?" Schruille asked.

"I'm sure," she said.

"Then we should've told him."

"And told him how we knew?" she asked.

"I know the argument," Schruille said. "Blunt the instrument, spoil the work."

"That Svengaard, he's one of the reliable ones," Nourse said.

"It is said we walk the sharp edge of a knife," Schruille said. "When you walk the knife, you must be careful *how* you place your feet."

"What a disgusting idea," Calapine said. She turned to Nourse. "Are you still hobbying da Vinci, dearest?"

"His brush stroke," Nourse said. "A most exacting discipline. I should have it in forty or fifty years. Soon at any rate."

"Provided you've placed each step correctly," Schruille said.

Presently, Nourse said, "Sometimes, Schruille, you allow cynicism to carry you beyond the bounds of propriety." He turned, studied the instrument gauges, sensors, peek-eyes and read-outs across from Calapine on the inner wall of the globe. "It's reasonably quiet today. Shall we leave the control with Schruille, Cal, and go down for a swim and a pharmacy session."

"Body tone, body tone," Schruille complained. "Have

you ever considered doing twenty-five laps of the pool instead of twenty?"

"You say the most astonishing things of late," Calapine said. "Would you have Nourse upset his enzyme balance? I fail completely in my attempts to understand you."

"Fail to try," Schruille said.

"Is there anything we can do for you?" she asked.

"My cycle has plunged me into dreadful monotony," Schruille said. "Is there something you can do about that?"

Nourse looked at Schruille in the prismatic reflector. The man's voice with its suggestion of a whine had grown increasingly annoying of late. Nourse was beginning to regret that community of tastes and bodily requirements had thrown them together. Perhaps when the Tuyere's service was done . . .

"Monotony," Calapine said. She shrugged.

"There's a certain triumph in well-considered monotony," Nourse said. "That's Voltaire, I believe."

"It sounded like the purest Nourse," Schruille said.

"I sometimes find it helpful," Calapine said, "to invoke a benign concern for the Folk."

"Even among ourselves?" Schruille asked.

"Consider the fate of the poor computer nurse," she said. "In the abstract, naturally. Can you not feel sorrow and pity?"

"Pity's a wasteful emotion," Schruille said. "Sorrow is akin to cynicism." He smiled. "This will pass. Go to your swim. When the vigor's on you, think of me . . . here."

Nourse and Calapine stood, ordered the carrier beams into position.

"Efficiency," Nourse said. "We must seek more efficiency in our minions. Things must be made to run more smoothly."

Schruille looked up at them waiting for the beams. He wanted only to be free of the wanton rambling of their voices. They missed the point, insisted on missing it.

"Efficiency?" Calapine asked. "Perhaps you're right."

Schruille no longer could contain the emotions at war

within him. "Efficiency's the opposite of craftsmanship,"
he said. "Think on that!"

The beams came. Nourse and Calapine slid down and
away without answering, leaving Schruille to close the segment. He sat alone at last within the green-blue-red winking
of the control center—alone except for the glittering eyes
of scanners activated along the upper circle of the globe.
He counted eighty-one of them alive and staring at him and
at the responses of the globe. Eighty-one of his fellows . . .
or groups of his fellows were out there observing him and
his work as he observed the Folk and their work.

The scanners imparted a vague uneasiness to Schruille.
Before the Tuyere's service, he could never remember
watching the control center or its activities. Too much that
was painful and unthinkable occurred here. Were the former masters of the control center curious about how the
new trio dispatched its duties? Who were the watchers?

Schruille dropped his attention to the instruments. In mo-
ments like this he often felt like Chen Tzu-ang's "Master
of Dark Truth" who saw the whole world in a jade bottle.
Here was the jade bottle—this globe. A flick of the power
ring on the arm of his throne and he could watch a couple
making love in Warsopolis, study the contents of an embryo vat in Greater London or loose hypnotic gas with tam-
ing suggestions into a warren of New Peking. The touch of
a key and he could analyze the shifting motives of an entire
work force in the megalopolis of Roma.

Searching within himself, Schruille could not find the
impulse to move a single control.

He thought back, trying to remember how many scanners
had watched the first years of the Tuyere's service. He was
sure it had never exceeded ten or twelve. But now—eighty-
one.

I should've warned them about Svengaard, he thought. *I
could've said that we shouldn't rely on the assumption
there's a special Providence for fools. Svengaard is a fool
who disturbs me.*

But Nourse and Calapine would have defended Svengaard. He knew it. They'd have insisted the man was re-

liable, honorable, loyal. They'd wager anything on it.

Anything? Schruille wondered. *Is there something they might not wager on Svengaard's loyalty?*

Schruille could almost hear Nourse pontificating, *"Our judgment of Svengaard is the correct one."*

And that, Schruille thought, *is what disturbs me. Svengaard worships us . . . as does Max. But worship is nine-tenths fear.*

In time, everything becomes fear.

Schruille looked up at the watching scanners, spoke aloud: "Time-time-time . . ."

Let that chew at their vitals, he thought.

7

The place was a pumping station for the sewage reclamation system of Seatac Megalopolis. It lay at the eleven hundred foot level on the spur line that sent by-product irrigation water into Grand Coulee system. A four-story box of sampling pipes, computer consoles and access cat-walks aglow with force-buoyed lights, it throbbed to the pulse of the giant turbines it controlled.

The Durants had come down through the personnel tubes during the evening rush hour, moving in easy random stages that insured they weren't followed and that they carried no tracer devices. Five inspection tubes had passed them as clean.

Still, they were careful to read the faces and actions of the people who jostled past. Most of the people were dull pages, hurried, intent on their own business. Occasionally, they exchanged a mutual reading-glance with another courier, or identified sub-officials with the fear goading them on Optiman errands.

No one noticed a couple in workman brown, their hands clasped, who emerged onto Catwalk Nine of the pumping station.

The Durants paused there to survey their surroundings. They were tired, elated and more than a little awed at having been summoned into the control core of the Parents Underground. The smell of hydrocarbons filled the air around them. Lizbeth sniffed.

Her silent conversation through their clasped hands carried overtones of tension. Harvey worked to reassure her.

"It's probably our Glisson we're to see," he said.

"There could be other Cyborgs with the same name," she said.

"Not likely."

He urged her out onto the catwalk, past a hover light. They took a left branching past two workmen reading Pitot gauges, their faces in odd shadows created by the lights from below.

Lizbeth felt the lonely exposure of their position, signaled, *"How can we be sure* they *aren't watching us here?"*

"This must be one of our places," he said. *"You know."*

"How can it be?"

"Route the scanners through editing computers," he said. *"The Opts see only what we want them to see then."*

"It's dangerous to feel sure of such things," she said. Then, *"Why have they summoned us?"*

"We'll know in a few minutes," he said.

The walk led through a dust-excluding lock port into a tool bunker, gray walls punctured by outlets for transmission tubes, the inevitable computer controls blinking, ticking, chuckling, whirring. The place smelled of a sweet oil.

As the port clanged shut behind the Durants, a figure came from their left and sat on a padded bench across from them.

The Durants stared silently, recognizing and repelled by the recognition. The figure's outline suggested neither man nor woman. It looked planted there in the seat, and as they watched, it pulled thin cables from pockets in its gray coveralls, plugged the cables into the computer wall.

Harvey brought his attention up to the square, deeply seamed face and the light gray eyes with their stare of blank directness, that coldly measured observation which was a trademark of the Cyborg.

"Glisson," Harvey said, "you summoned us?"

"I summoned you," the Cyborg said. "It has been many years, Durant. Do you still fear us? I see that you do. You are late."

"We're unfamiliar with this area," Harvey said.

"We came carefully," Lizbeth said.

"Then I taught you well," Glisson said. "You were reasonably good pupils."

Through their clasped hands, Lizbeth signaled *"They're so hard to read, but something's wrong."* She averted her eyes from the Cyborg, chilled by the weighted stare. No matter how she tried to think of them as flesh and blood, her mind could never evade the knowledge that such bodies contained miniaturized computers linked directly to the brain, that the arms were not arms but prosthetic tools and weapons. And the voice—always such a clipped-off unemotional quality.

"You should not fear us, madam," Glisson said. "Unless you are not Lizbeth Durant."

Harvey failed to repress the snap of anger, said, "Don't talk to her that way! You don't own us."

"What is the first lesson I taught you after you were recruited?" Glisson asked.

Harvey brought himself under control, forced a rueful smile onto his mouth. "To hold our tempers," he said. Lizbeth's hand continued to tremble in his.

"That lesson you did not learn well," Glisson said. "I overlook your fallibility."

Through their hands, Lizbeth signaled, *"It was prepared for violence against us."*

Harvey acknowledged.

"First," Glisson said, "you will report on the genetic operation." There was a pause while the Cyborg changed its jacked connections to the computer wall. "Do not be distracted by my work. I distribute tools—thus"—it indicated the bunker—"this space which appears on *their* screens as a space filled with tools, will never be investigated."

A bench slid from the wall to the Durants' right. "If you are fatigued, sit," Glisson said. The Cyborg indicated its cable linkage to the wall computer. "I sit only that I may carry on the work of this space while we speak." The Cyborg smiled, a stiff rictus to signify that the Durants must realize such as Glisson did not feel fatigue.

Harvey urged Lizbeth to the bench. She sat as he signaled, *"Caution. Glisson's maneuvering us. Something's being hidden."*

Glisson turned slightly to face them, said, "A verbal, factual, complete report. Leave out nothing, no matter how trivial it may seem to you. I have limitless capacity for data."

They began recounting what they had observed of the genetic operation, taking up from each other on cue without a break as good couriers were taught to do. Harvey experienced the odd feeling during the recital that he and Lizbeth became part of the Cyborg's mechanism. Questions came so mechanically from Glisson's lips. Their answers felt so clinical. He had to keep reminding himself, *This is our son we discuss.*

Presently, Glisson said, "There seems no doubt we've another viable immune to the gas. Your evidence virtually completes the picture. We have other data, you know."

"I didn't know the surgeon was one of us," Lizbeth said.

There was a pause while Glisson's eyes went even blanker than usual. The Durants felt they could almost see the esoteric formulae flitting through Glisson's thinking-banks. It was said the Cyborgs composed most of their thoughts only in higher math, translating to common language as it suited them.

"The surgeon was not one of us," Glisson said. "But he soon will be."

What strategic formula produced those words, Harvey wondered. "What about the computer tape on the operation?" he asked.

"It's destroyed," Glisson said. "Even now, your embryo is being removed to a safe place. You will join him soon." A mechanical chuckle escaped the Cyborg's lips.

Lizbeth shivered. Harvey felt the tension of her through their hands. He said, "Is our son safe?"

"Safe," Glisson said. "Our plans insure that safety."

"How?" Lizbeth asked.

"You will understand soon," Glisson said. "An ancient and reliable way of safe concealment. Be assured: viables are valuable weapons. We do not risk our valuable weapons."

Lizbeth signaled, *"The cut—ask now."*

Harvey wet his lips with his tongue, said, "There are . . . when a Central surgeon's called in, usually it means the embryo could be cut to Optiman. Did they . . . is our son . . ."

Glisson's nostrils flared. The face took on a look of hauteur that said such ignorance insulted a Cyborg. The clipped voice said, "We would require a complete tape record, including the enzymic data even to guess. The tape is gone. Only the surgeon knows the result of the operation for certain. We have yet to question him."

Lizbeth said: "Svengaard or the computer nurse might've said something that—"

"Svengaard is a dolt," Glisson said. "The computer nurse is dead."

"They killed her?" Lizbeth whispered.

"How she died isn't important," Glisson said. "She served her purpose."

With his hand, Harvey signaled, *"The Cyborgs had something to do with her death!"*

"I saw," she answered.

Harvey said, "Are you . . . will we be allowed to talk to Potter?"

"Potter will be offered full Cyborg status," Glisson said. "Talking will be his decision . . . afterward."

"We want to know about our son!" Lizbeth flared.

Harvey signaled frantically, *"Apologize!"*

"Madam," Glisson said, "let me remind you the so-called Optiman cut is not a state to which we aspire. Remember your vows."

She squeezed Harvey's hand to silence his signals, said, "I'm sorry. It was such a shock to learn . . . the possibility . . ."

"Your emotional excesses are taken into account as a mitigating circumstance," Glisson said. "It is well, therefore, that I warn you of a thing to happen. You will hear things about your son which you must *not* let excite you."

"What things?" Lizbeth whispered.

"An outside force of unknown origin sometimes interferes with the anticipated course of a genetic operation," Glisson said. "There is reason to believe this happened with your son."

"What do you mean?" Harvey asked.

"Mean!" Glisson sneered. "You ask questions to which there are no answers."

"What does this . . . *thing* do?" Lizbeth supplied.

Glisson looked at her. "It behaves somewhat in the fashion of a charged particle, penetrates the genetic core and alters the structure. If this has happened to your son, you may consider it beneficial because it apparently prevents the Optiman cut."

The Durants digested this.

Presently, Harvey said, "Do you require more of us? May we go now?"

"You will remain here," Glisson said.

They stared.

"You will wait for further orders," Glisson said.

"But we'll be missed," Lizbeth said. "Our apartment, they'll—"

"We've raised dopplegangers to play your roles long enough for you to escape Seatac," Glisson said. "You can never go back. You should've known this."

Harvey's lips moved, then, "Escape? What's . . . why are . . ."

"There is violence," Glisson said. "Even now. The death-wish cults will have their day." The Cyborg raised its gaze toward the ceiling. "War . . . blood . . . killing. It will be as it was before when the skies flamed and the earth ran molten."

Harvey cleared his throat. *Wars . . . before.* Glisson gave the impression that wars had been recent, perhaps only yesterday. And for this Cyborg that might be true. It was said that Glisson's grandsire had fought in the Optiman-Cyborg war. No one of the Underground Folk knew how many identities Glisson had lived.

"Where'll we go?" Harvey asked. He signaled Lizbeth not to interrupt.

"A place has been prepared," Glisson said.

The Cyborg arose, unplugged its linkage with the computer panel, said, "You will wait here. Do not attempt to leave. Your needs will be provided for."

Glisson left by the lock port and it sealed with a heavy thump.

"They're as bad as the Optimen," Lizbeth signaled.

"The day will come when we're free of both them and the Opts," Harvey said.

"It'll never happen," she said.

"Don't say that!" he ordered.

"If only we knew a friendly surgeon," she said. *"We could take our son and run."*

"That's foolishness! How could we service the vat without machinery for—"

"I've that machinery right inside me," she said. *"I was . . . born with it."*

Harvey stared at her, shocked speechless.

"I don't want the Cyborgs or the Opts controlling our son's life," she said, *"regulating his mind with hypnotic gas, making duplicates of him for their own purposes, pushing him and leading him and—"*

"Don't work yourself into a state," he said.

"You heard him," she said. *"Dopplegangers! They can regulate anything—our very being! They can condition us to . . . to . . . do anything! For all we know, we've been conditioned to be here right now!"*

"Liz, you're being unreasonable."

"Unreasonable? Look at me! They can take a piece of my skin and grow an identical copy. Me! Identical! How do you know I'm me? How do you know I'm the original me? How do I know?"

He gripped her free arm and for a moment had no words.

Presently, he forced himself to relax, shook his head. *"You're you, Liz. You're not flesh grown from a cell. You're . . . all the things we've shared . . . and been . . . and done together. They couldn't duplicate memories . . . not that with a doppleganger."*

She pressed her cheek against the rough fabric of his jacket, wanting the comfort of it, the tactile sensation that told her body he was here and he was real.

"They'll make dopplegangers of our son," she said. *"That's what they're planning. You know it."*

"Then we'll have many sons."

"For what reason?" She looked up at him, her lashes damp with unshed tears. *"You heard what Glisson said. Something from outside adjusted our embryo. What was it?"*

"How can I know?"

"Somebody must know."

"I know you," he said. *"You want to think it's God."*

"What else could it be?"

"Anything—chance, accident, some higher order manipulator. Maybe someone's discovered something they're not sharing."

"One of us? They wouldn't!"

"Nature, then," he said. *"Nature asserting itself in the interest of Man."*

"Sometimes you sound like a cultist!"

"It isn't the Cyborgs," he said. *"We know that."*

"Glisson said it was beneficent."

"But it's genetic shaping. That's blasphemy to them. Physical alteration of the bioframe, that's their way."

"Like Glisson," she said. *"That robot with flesh."* Again, she pressed her cheek against him. *"That's what I fear— they'll do that to our son . . . our sons."*

"The courier service outnumbers the Cyborgs a hundred to one," he said. *"As long as we stick together, we'll win."*

"But we're just flesh," she said, *"and so weak."*

"And we can do something all those Sterries together can't do," he reminded her. *"We can perpetuate our own kind."*

"What does it matter?" she asked. *"Optimen never die."*

8

Svengaard waited for night and checked the area through the observation screens in his office before going down to the vat room. In spite of the fact that this was *his* hospital and he had a perfect right here, he was conscious of doing a forbidden thing. The significance of the interview at Central hadn't escaped him. The Optimen wouldn't like this, but he had to look in that vat.

He paused in the darkness of the vat room, stood there near the door, realizing with a sense of detachment that he had never before been in here without the full blaze of lights. There were only the glow bulbs behind gauges and telltales now—faint dots and circles of luminescence by which to orient himself.

The *thrap-thrap-thrap* of viapumps created an odd contrapuntal rhythm which filled the gloom with a sense of urgency. Svengaard imagined all the embryos in there (twenty-one at the morning count) their cells reaching out, doubling and redoubling and re-redoubling in the strange ecstasy of growth—becoming unique, distinct, discrete individuals.

Not for them the contraceptive gas that permeated Folk breathing spaces. Not yet. Now, they could grow almost as their ancestors had grown before the genetic engineers.

Svengaard sniffed.

His nostrils, instinctively alerted by the darkness, sensed the amniotic saltiness of the air. From its odor, this room could almost have been a primal seashore with life burgeoning in its ooze.

Svengaard shuddered and reminded himself, *I'm a submolecular engineer, a gene surgeon. There's nothing strange here.*

But the thought failed to convince him.

He pushed himself away from the door, headed down the line looking for the vat with the Durant embryo. In his mind lay the clear memory of what he had seen in that embryo— the intrusion that had flooded the cells with arginine. Intrusion. Where had it originated? Was Potter correct? Was it an unknown creator of stability? Stability . . . order . . . systems. Extended systems . . . infinite aspects of energy that left all matter insubstantial.

These suddenly were frightening thoughts here in the whispering gloom.

He stumbled against a low instrument stand, cursed softly. His stomach felt tight with the urgency of the via-pumps and the real urgency in the fact that he had to finish here before the duty nurse made her hourly rounds.

An insect shape, shadow against shadows, stood out against the wall in front of him. He froze and it took a moment for him to recognize the familiar outlines of the meson microscope.

Svengaard turned to the luminous numbers on the vats— twelve, thirteen, fourteen . . . fifteen. Here it was. He checked the name on the tag, reading it in the glow of a gauge bulb: "Durant."

Something about this embryo had the Optimen upset and Security in an uproar. His regular computer nurse was gone—where, nobody could say. The replacement walked like a man.

Svengaard wheeled out the microscope, moving gently in the darkness, positioned the instrument over the vat, made the connections by feel. The vat throbbed against his fingers. He rigged for scanning, bent to the viewer.

Up out of the swarming cellular mass came a hydrophilic gene segment. He centered on it, the darkness forgotten as he pushed his awareness into the scope-lighted field of the viewer. Meson probes slid down . . . down into the mitochondrial structure. He found the alphahelices and began checking out polypeptide chains.

A puzzled frown creased his brow. He switched to another cell. Another.

The cells were low in arginine—he could see that. Thoughts brushed their way through his mind as he peered and hunted, *How could the Durant embryo, of all embryos, be low on arginine? Any normal male would have more sperm protamine than this. How could the ADP-ATP exchange system carry no hint of Optiman? The cut wouldn't make this much difference.*

Abruptly, Svengaard sent his probes down into the sex identifiers, scanned the overlapping helices.

Female!

He straightened, checked number and tag. "Fifteen. Durant."

Svengaard bent to the inspection chart, read it in the gauge glow. It showed the duty nurse's notations for the eighty-first hour. He glanced at his watch: still twenty minutes before she made the eighty-second hour check.

The Durant embryo could not possibly be female, he thought. *Not from Potter's operation.*

Someone had switched embryos, he realized. One embryo would activate the vat's life-system responses much like another. Without microscopic examination, the change couldn't be detected.

Who?

In Svengaard's mind, the most likely candidates were the Optimen. They'd removed the Durant embryo to a safe place and left a substitute.

Why?

Bait, he thought. *Bait.*

Who are they trying to catch?

He straightened, mouth dry, heart pumping rapidly. A sound at the wall to his left brought him whirling around.

The vat room's emergency computer panel had come to life, tapes beginning to turn, lights winking. A read-out board clattered.

But there was no operator!

Svengaard whirled to run from the room, collided with a blocky, unmoving shape. Arms and hands gripped him with unmerciful pressure and he saw beyond his captor a section of the vat room wall open with dim light there and movement.

Then darkness exploded in his skull.

9

Seatac Hospital's new computer nurse got Max Allgood on the phone after only a short delay while Security traced him. Allgood's eyes appeared sunken. His mouth was pulled into a thin line.

"Yes?" he said. "Oh, it's you."

"Something important's come up," she said. "Svengaard's in the vat room examining the Durant embryo under microscope."

Allgood rolled his eyes. "Oh, for the love . . . Is that why you got me out of . . . is that why you called me?"

"But there was a noise and you said—"

"Forget it."

"I tell you there was a commotion of some kind in that room and now Doctor Svengaard's gone. I didn't see him go."

"He probably left by another door."

"There is no other door."

"Look, sweetie, I have half a hundred agents there covering that room like a blanket. A fly couldn't move in that room without our scanners picking it up."

"Then check with them to see where Svengaard's gone."

"Oh, for—"

"Check!"

"All right!" Allgood turned to his hot line, got the duty agent. The computer nurse could hear him through her open line. "Where's Svengaard?"

A muffled voice responded, "Just went in and examined the Durant embryo under microscope, then left."

"Went out the door?"

"Just walked out."

Allgood's face came back onto the computer nurse's screen. "You hear that?"

"I heard, but I've been down at the end of the hall ever since he went in. He didn't come out."

"You probably turned your back for five seconds."

"Well . . ."

"You did, didn't you?"

"I may've looked away just for a second, but—"

"So you missed him."

"But I heard a commotion in there!"

"If there was anything wrong, my men would've reported it. Now, forget this. Svengaard's no problem. *They* said he'd probably do this and we could ignore it. They're never wrong about such things."

"If you're sure."

"I'm sure."

"Say, why are we so interested in that embryo?"

"You don't need to know, sweetie. Get back to work and let me get some sleep."

She broke the connection, still wondering about the noise she had heard. It had sounded like something being hit.

Allgood sat staring at the blank screen after the nurse signed off. *Noise? Commotion?* He formed a circle with his mouth, exhaled slowly. *Crazy damn' female!*

Abruptly, he stood up, turned back to his bed. The doxie playmate he'd brought in for the night lay there in the rosy light of a gloom dispeller, half awake, looking at him. Her eyes under long lashes filled him with sudden rage.

"Get the hell out of here!" he roared.

She sat upright in the bed, wide awake, staring.

"Out!" he said, pointing to the door.

She tumbled out of bed, grabbed her clothing and ran out the door, a flash of pink flesh.

Only when she'd gone did Allgood realize who she'd reminded him of—Calapine, a dull Calapine. He wondered at himself then. The Cyborg had said the adjustments they made, the instruments they'd implanted, would help him control his emotions, permit him to lie with impunity even to Optimen. This outburst now—it frightened him. He stared down at one of his slippers abandoned on the gray rug, its mate vanished somewhere. He kicked the slipper, began pacing back and forth.

Something was wrong. He could feel it. He'd lived almost four hundred *lovely* years, most of them in Optiman service. He had a well-trained instinct for rightness and wrongness. It was survival.

Something was wrong.

Had the Cyborg lied to him? Was he being used for some trick of their own?

He stumbled over the slipper, ignored it.

Noise. Commotion.

With a low curse, he returned to the hot line, got his duty agent. The man's face on the screen looked like an infant's—puffy lips and big, eager eyes.

"Go down to that vat room and inspect it," Allgood said. "The fine tooth. Look for signs of a commotion."

"But if anybody sees us—"

"Damn it to hell! Do as I say!"

"Yes, sir!"

The agent clicked off.

Allgood threw off his robe, all thought of sleep forgotten, ran through a quick shower and began dressing.

Something was wrong. He could feel it. Before leaving his quarters he put out a call to have Svengaard picked up and brought in for questioning.

10

By eight A.M., the streets and speedwalks of Seatac's industrial district-north swarmed with machine and foot traffic—the jostling impersonals of people following the little strung-out channels of their private concerns. Weather control had said the day would be held to a comfortable seventy-eight Fahrenheit with no clouds. An hour from now as the day settled into its working tempo, traffic would become more sparse. Dr. Potter had seen the city at that pace many times, but he had never before been immersed in the shift-break swarm.

He was aware that the Parents Underground had chosen this time for its natural concealment. He and his guide were just two more impersonals here. Who would notice them? This didn't subtract, though, from his fascinated interest in a scene that was new to him.

A big female Sterrie in the green-white striped uniform of a machine-press operator in the heavy industry complex pushed past him. She looked to Potter like a B2022419^{k}G8 cut with cream skin and heavy features. In a gold loop in her right ear she wore a dancing doll breeder fetish.

Almost in lock step behind her trotted a short man with hunched-up shoulders carrying a short brass rod. He flashed an impish grin at Potter as they passed, as much as to say:

"Here's the only way to get through a crowd like this."

Potter's guide turned Potter aside onto the step-down walk and then into a side street. The guide was an enigma to Potter, who couldn't place the cut. The man wore a plain brown service suit, coveralls. He appeared reasonably normal except for a pale, almost sickly skin. His deeply set eyes glittered almost like lenses. A skull cap concealed his hair except for a few dark brown strands that looked almost artificial. His hands when they touched Potter to guide him felt cold and faintly repellent.

The crowd thinned here as the step-down walk rounded a corner into a byway canyon between two towering windowless buildings. There was dust in this cavernous street rising up and almost concealing a distant tracery of bridges. Potter wondered at the dust. It was as though the director of local weather allowed dust here in an unconscious passion for naturalness.

A bulky man hurried past them and Potter was caught by the look of his hands—thick wrists, bulging knuckles, horned callouses. He had no idea what work could cause such deformity.

The guide steered them now onto a succession of drop walks and into the cave of an alley. The swarm was left behind. A feeling of detachment seized Potter. He felt he was re-living an old and familiar experience.

Why did I come with this person? he wondered.

The guide wore the wheeled blazon of a transport driver on his shoulder, but he'd said right out he was from the Parents Underground.

"I know what you did for us," he'd said. "Now, we will do something for you." A turn of the head. "Come."

They'd talked only briefly after that, but Potter had known from the first the guide had correctly identified himself. This was no trick.

Then why did I accept the invitation? Potter asked himself. Certainly it wasn't for the veiled promises of extended life and instant knowledge. There were Cyborgs behind this, of course, and he suspected this guide might be one of them. Most of the Optimen and Servant Uppers tended to discount the Folk rumors that Cyborgs did exist, but Potter had never joined the cynics and scoffers. He could no more explain why than he could explain his presence here in this alley cave walking between dark plasmeld walls illuminated by the ghost flicker of overhead glowtubes.

Potter suspected he had at last rebelled against one of the three curses of their age—moderation, drugs and alcohol. Narco-pleasures and alcohol had tempted him in their time . . . and finally moderation. He knew it wasn't normal for the times. Better to take up with one of the wild sex cults. But pointless sex without even the faint hope of issue had palled on him, although he knew this for a sign of final dissolution.

The alley opened into one of the lost squares of the megalopolis—a triangular paving and fountain that looked to be real stone, green with the slime of ages.

The Optimen don't know about this place, Potter thought. They despised stone which eroded and wore away—in their time. Regenerative plasmeld was the thing. It stood unmoved and unmoving for all time.

The guide slowed as they reached the open air. Potter noted a faint smell of chemicals about the man, oily sweetness, and a tiny scar running diagonally down the back of his neck into his collar.

Why didn't he try to blackmail me into coming? Potter wondered. *Could he be that sure? Could anyone know me that well?*

"We have a job for you," the guide had said. "An operation you must perform."

Curiosity is my weakness, Potter thought. *That's why I'm here.*

The guide put a hand on Potter's arm, said, "Stop. Wait without moving."

The tone was conversational, calm, but Potter felt hidden tensions. He looked up and around. The buildings were windowless, faceless. A wide door stood out in the angle of another alleyway ahead. They had come almost around the fountain without encountering another person. Nothing stirred or moved around them. There was only the faint rumbling of distant machinery.

"What is it?" Potter whispered. "Why're we waiting?"

"Nothing," the guide said. "Wait."

Potter shrugged.

His mind veered back to the first encounter with this creature. *How could they know what I achieved with that embryo? It must be the computer nurse. She's one of them.*

The guide had refused to say.

I came because I hoped they could help me solve the mystery of the Durant embryo, he thought. *They were the source of the arginine intrusion—that's what I suspect.*

He thought of Svengaard's description—a contrail-like intrusion. It had deposited arginine-rich sperm protamine through the coiled alpha-helices of the embryo's cells. Then had come the operation—the cysteine masked, neutralized with sulfhydryl and the ATP phase . . . oligomycin and azide . . . the exchange reaction inhibited.

Potter stared up at the patch of blue sky framed by the buildings around the square. His mind, concentrated on the Durant cutting, had encountered a new idea. He no longer saw the sky. His awareness was back within the swarming cell structure, following the mitochondrial systems like an undersea hunter.

"It could be repeated," Potter whispered.

"Silence," the guide hissed.

Potter nodded. *On any embryo at all,* he thought. *The key's the arginine flooding. I could duplicate that myself on the basis of Sven's description. Gods! We could make billions of Durant embryos! And every one of them self-viable!*

He took a deep breath, dismayed by the realization that—with the record tape erased—his memory might be the only container of that entire operation and its implications. Svengaard and the computer nurse could have only part of it. They hadn't been *in* there, immersed in the heart of the cell.

A brilliant surgeon might deduce what had happened and be able to reproduce the operation from the partial records, but only if he were set the problem. Who would ever take up this problem? Not the Optimen. Not that dolt Svengaard.

The guide tugged at Potter's arm.

Potter looked down into that flat, chill-eyed face with its lack of genetic identification.

"We are observed," the guide said in an oddly depersonalized tone. "Listen to me very carefully. Your life depends on it."

Potter shook his head, blinked. He felt removed from his own person, become only a set of senses to record this man's words and actions.

"You will go through that door ahead of us," the guide said.

Potter turned, looked at the door. Two men carrying paper-wrapped parcels emerged from the alley in front of it, hurried around the square opposite them. The guide ignored them. Potter heard a babble of young voices growing louder in the alley. The guide ignored these, too.

"Inside that building, you will take the first door on your left," he said. "You will see a woman there operating a voicebox. You will say to her: 'My shoe pinches.' She will say: 'Everyone has troubles.' She will take care of you from there."

Potter found his voice: "What if . . . she's not there?"

"Then go through the door behind her desk and out through the adjoining office into a rear hall. Turn left and go to the rear of the building. You will find there a man in a loader supervisor's uniform, striped gray and black. You will repeat the procedure with him."

"What about you?" Potter asked.

"That is not your concern. Quickly, now!" The guide gave him a push.

Potter stumbled toward the door just as a woman in a teacher's uniform emerged from the alley leading a file of children between him and the bolt hole.

Potter's shocked senses took in the scene—children, all dressed in tight shorts that revealed their long flamingo legs. They were all around him suddenly and he was bulling his way through toward the door.

Behind him, someone screamed.

Potter lurched against the door, found the handle, looked back.

His guide had gone around to the opposite side of the fountain which concealed him now from the waist down, but what remained visible was enough to make Potter gasp and freeze. The man's chest was bare revealing a single milky white dome from which blazed a searing light.

Potter turned left, saw a line of men emerging from another alley to be crisped and burned down by that searing light. The children were shouting, crying, falling back into the alley from which they had emerged, but Potter ignored them, fascinated by this slaughter-machine which he'd thought was a human being.

One of the guide's arms lifted, pointed overhead. From the extended fingers, lancets of searing blue stabbed upward. Where the light terminated, aircars tumbled from the sky. The air all around had become an ozone-crackling inferno punctuated by explosions, screams, hoarse shouts.

Potter stood there watching, unable to move, forgetful of his instructions or the door or his hand upon the door's handle.

Return fire was coming now at the guide. His clothing shriveled, vanished in smoke to reveal an armored body with muscles that had to be plasmeld fibers. The ravening beams continued to blaze from his hands and chest.

Potter found he no longer could bear to watch. He wrenched the door open, stumbled through into the relative gloom of a yellow-walled foyer. He slammed the door behind him as an explosion rocked the building. The door rattled behind him.

On his left, a door was flung open. A tiny blue-eyed blonde woman stood there staring at him. Potter found himself oddly recognizing the markers of her genetic cut, reassured by the touch of humanity in these tiny betrayals. He could see the cabinet of a voicebox in the room behind her.

"My shoe pinches," Potter said.

She gulped. "Everyone has troubles."

"I am Dr. Potter," he said. "I think my escort has just been killed."

She stepped aside, said, "In here."

Potter lurched past her into an office with lines of empty desks. His mind was a turmoil. He felt shaken to his roots by the implications of the violence he had just witnessed.

The woman took his arm, herded him toward another door. "Through here," she said. "We'll have to go into the service tubes. That's the only way. They'll have this place surrounded in minutes."

Potter stopped, figuratively dug in his heels. He hadn't counted on violence. He didn't know what he had expected, but not that.

"Where're we going?" he demanded. "Why do you want me?"

"Don't you know?" she asked.

"He . . . never said."

"Everything'll be explained," she said. "Hurry."

"I don't move a millimeter until you tell me," he said.

A raw street oath escaped her lips. She said, "If I must I must. You're to implant the Durant embryo in its mother. It's the only way we can get it out of here."

"*In* the mother?"

"In the ancient way," she said. "I know it's disgusting, but it's the only way. Now, hurry!"

Potter allowed himself to be herded through the door.

11

In the control center, their red Survey Globe, the Tuyere occupied the thrones on the pivoting triangle, reviewing data and reviewing data—correlating, deducing, commanding. The 120-degree scan of curved wall available to each of them flashed with data in numerous modes—pictorially in the spying screens, as probability function in mathematical read-outs, as depth-module decision analogues, as superior/inferior unit apportionments pictured in free-flowing pyramids, as visual reports reduced to cubed grids of binaries according to relative values, as motivational curves weighted for action/reaction and presented in flowing green lines . . .

In the upper quadrants, scanner eyes glittered to show how many of the Optimen were sitting in on the globe's activity—over a thousand this morning.

Calapine worried the prescription ring on her left thumb, felt the abortive hum of power in it as she twisted and slid it along her skin. She was restless, full of demands for which she could find no names. The duties of the globe were becoming repellent, her companions hateful. In here, time settled into more of a continuous blur without days or nights. Every companion she had ever known grew to be the same companion, merged, endlessly merged.

"Once more have I studied the protein synthesis tape on the Durant embryo," Nourse said. He glanced at Calapine in the reflector beside his head, drummed the arm of his throne with fingers that moved back and forth, back and forth on the carved plasmeld.

"Something we've missed, something we've missed," Calapine mocked. She looked at Schruille, caught him rubbing his hands along his robe at his thighs, a motion that seemed filled with stark betrayal of nervousness.

"Now it happens I've discovered the thing we missed," Nourse said.

A movement of Schruille's head caught Nourse's attention. He turned. For a moment, they stared at each other in the prisms. Nourse found it interesting that Schruille betrayed a tiny skin blemish beside his nose.

Odd, Nourse thought. *How could one of us have a blemish such as that? Surely there could be no enzymic imbalance.*

"Well, what is it?" Schruille demanded.

"You've a blemish beside your nose," Nourse said.

Schruille stared at him.

"You deduce this from the embryo's tape?" Calapine asked.

"Eh? Oh . . . no, of course not."

"Then what is it you've discovered?"

"Yes. Well . . . it seems rather obvious now that the operation Potter performed may be repeatable—given that general type of embryo and proper administration of sperm protamine."

Schruille shuddered.

"Have you deduced the course of the operation?" Calapine asked.

"Not precisely, but in outline, yes."

"Potter could repeat it?" she asked.

"Perhaps even Svengaard."

"Guard and preserve us," Calapine muttered. It was a ritual formula whose words seldom caught an Optiman's conscious attention, but she heard herself this time and the word "preserve" stood out as though outlined in fire.

She whirled away.

"Where is Max?" Schruille asked.

The whine in Schruille's voice brought a sneer to Nourse's lips.

"Max is working," Nourse said. "He is busy."

Schrille looked up at the watching scanners, thinking of all their fellows behind those lensed eyes—the Actionists seeing events as a new demand upon their talents, not realizing what violence might be unleashed here; the Emotionals, fearful and complaining, rendered almost ineffective by guilt feelings; the Cynics, interested by the new *game* (most of the watchers, Schruille felt, were Cynics); the Hedonists, angered by the current sense of urgent emergency, worried because such matters interfered with their enjoyments; and the Effetes, looking in all this for something new at which to sneer.

Will we now develop a new party? Schruille asked himself. *Will we now have the Brutals, all sensitivity immured by the needs of self-preservation? Nourse and Calapine haven't faced this as yet.*

Again, he shuddered.

"Max calls," Calapine said. "I have him in my transient screen."

Schruille and Nourse flicked their channel duplicators, looked down at Allgood's swarthy, solid, muscular figure in the transient screen.

"I report," Allgood said.

Calapine watched the Security chief's face. He appeared oddly distracted, fearful.

"What of Potter?" Nourse asked.

Allgood blinked.

"Why does he delay his answer?" Schruille asked.

"It's because he worships us," Calapine said.

"Worship is a product of fear," Schruille said. "Perhaps there's something he wishes to show us, a projection or an evidential sub-datum. Is that it, Max?"

Allgood stared out of the screen, looking from one to the other. They'd gotten tied up in that lost-time sense again, the endless word play and disregard for time in the quest for data, data, data—that side effect of endless life, the supra-involvement in trivia. This time, he hoped it would go on without end.

"Where is Potter?" Nourse demanded.

Allgood swallowed. "Potter has . . . temporarily eluded us." He knew better than to lie or evade now.

"Eluded?" Schruille asked.

"How?" Nourse asked.

"There was . . . violence," Allgood said.

"Show us this violence," Schruille said.

"No," Calapine said. "I will take Max's word for it."

"Do you doubt Max?" Nourse asked.

"No doubts," Schruille said. "But I will see this violence."

"How can you?" Calapine asked.

"Leave if you wish," Schruille said. He measured out his words: "I . . . will . . . see . . . this . . . violence." He looked at Allgood. "Max?"

Allgood swallowed. This was a development he had not anticipated.

"It happened," Nourse said. "We know that, Schruille."

"Of course it happened," Schruille said. "I saw the mark where it was edited out of our channels. Violence. Now, I wish to bypass the safety valve which protects our sensitivities." He snorted. "Sensitivities!"

Nourse stared at him, noting that all traces of a whine had gone from Schruille's voice.

Schruille looked up at the scanners, saw that many were winking off. He was disgusting even the Cynics, no doubt. A few remained, though.

Will they stay through to the end? he wondered.

"Show the violence, Max," Schruille ordered.

Allgood shrugged.

Nourse swiveled his throne around, putting his back to the screen. Calapine put her hands over her eyes.

"As you command," Allgood said. His face vanished from the screen, was replaced by a high view looking down into a tiny square between windowless buildings. Two tiny figures walked around a fountain in the square. They stopped and a close-up showed the faces—Potter and an unknown, a strange-looking man with frighteningly cold eyes.

Again, the long view—two other men emerging from an alley carrying paper-wrapped packages. Behind them trooped a file of children with adult monitor in teacher's uniform.

Abruptly, Potter was lurching, pushing through the children. His companion was running the other way around the fountain.

Schruille risked a glance at Calapine, caught her peeking between her fingers.

A shrill, piercing cry from the screen, brought his attention jerking back.

Potter's companion had become a thing of horror, clothing fallen away, a milky bulb arising from his chest to flare with brilliant light.

The screen went blank, came alive again to a view from a slightly different angle.

A quick glance showed that Calapine had dropped all pretense of hiding her eyes, was staring at the screen. Nourse, too, watched through his shoulder prism.

Another blaze of light leaped from the figure in the screen. Again the scene went blank.

"It's a Cyborg," Schruille said. "Know that as you watch."

Again, the scene came alive from a different angle and this time from very high. The action in the plasmeld canyon was reduced to a movement of midges, but there was no difficulty in finding the center of violence. Lancets of blazing light leaped upward from a lurching figure in the square. Aircars exploded and fell from the sky in pieces.

One Security vehicle plummeted in behind the Cyborg. A pulsing beam of coherent light emerged from it to cut a smoking furrow down the side of a building. The Cyborg whirled, lifted a hand from which a blinding blue finger seemed to extend into infinity. The finger met the diving car, split it in half. One half hit a building, ricocheted and smashed into the Cyborg.

A ball of yellow brilliance took shape in the square. In a second, a reverberating explosion shook the scene.

Schruille looked up to find the circle of watching scanners complete, every lensed eye blazing red.

Calapine cleared her throat. "Potter went into that building on the right."

"Is that all you can say?" Schruille asked.

Nourse swiveled his throne, glared at Schruille.

"Was it not interesting?" Schruille asked.

"Interesting?" Nourse demanded.

"It is called warfare," Schruille said.

Allgood's face reappeared on the screen, looking up at them with a veiled intensity.

He's naturally curious at our reaction, Schruille thought.

"Do you know of *our* weapons, Max?" Schruille asked.

"This talk of weapons and violence disgusts me," Nourse said. "What is the good of this?"

"Why do we have weapons if they were not intended for use?" Schruille asked. "Do you know the answer, Max?"

"I know of your weapons," Allgood said. "They are the ultimate safeguard for your persons."

"Of course we have weapons!" Nourse shouted. "But why must we—"

"Nourse, you demean yourself," Calapine said.

Nourse pushed himself back in his throne, hands gripping the arms. *"Demean myself!"*

"Let us review this new development," Schruille said. "Cyborgs we knew existed. They have eluded us consistently. Thus, they control computer editing channels and have sympathy among the Folk. Thus, we see, they have an Action Arm which can sacrifice . . . I say *sacrifice* a member for the good of the whole."

Nourse stared at him, wide-eyed, drinking the words.

"And we," Schruille said, "we had forgotten how to be thoroughly brutal."

"Faaah!" Nourse barked.

"If you injure a man with a weapon," Schruille said, "which is the responsible party—the weapon or the one who wields it?"

"Explain yourself," Calapine whispered.

Schruille pointed to Allgood in the screen. "There is our weapon. We've wielded it times without number until it learned to wield itself. We've not forgotten how to be brutal, we've merely forgotten that we *are* brutal."

"What rot!" Nourse said.

"Look," Schruille said. He pointed up to the watching scanners, every one of them alive. "There's my evidence," Schruille said. "When have so many watched in the globe?"

A few of the lights began to wink out, but came back as the channels were taken over by other watchers.

Allgood watching from the screen felt the thrill of complete fascination. A tight sensation in his chest prevented deep breaths, but he ignored it. The Optimen facing violence! After a lifetime playing with euphemisms, Allgood found the thought of this almost unacceptable. It had been so swift. But then these were the live-forevers, the people who could not fail. He wondered then at the thoughts which raced through their minds.

Schruille, the usually silent and watchful, looked down at Allgood and said, "Who else has eluded us, Max?"

Allgood found himself unable to speak.

"The Durants are missing," Schruille said. "Svengaard has not been found. Who else?"

"No one, Schruille. No one."

"We want them captured," Schruille said.

"Of course, Schruille."

"Alive," Calapine said.

"Alive, Calapine?" Allgood asked.

"If it's possible," Schruille said.

Allgood nodded. "I obey, Schruille."

"You may get back to your work now," Schruille said.

The screen went blank.

Schruille busied himself with the controls in the arm of his throne.

"What're you doing?" Nourse demanded and he heard the petulance in his own voice, despising it.

"I remove the censors which excluded violence from our

eyes except as a remote datum," Schruille said. "It is time we observed the reality of our land."

Nourse sighed. "If you feel it's necessary."

"I know it's necessary."

"Most interesting," Calapine said.

Nourse looked at her. "What do you find interesting in this obscenity?"

"This exhilaration I feel," she said. "It's most interesting."

Nourse whirled away from her, glared at Schruille. He could see now that there definitely was a skin blemish on Schruille's face—beside his nose.

12

To Svengaard, raised in the ordered world of the Optimen, the idea that they were fallible came as heresy. He tried to put it out of his mind and his ears. To be fallible was to be subject to death. Only the lower orders suffered thus. Not the Optimen. How could they be fallible?

He knew the surgeon sitting across from him in the pale dawn light that filtered through narrow slots in a domed ceiling. The man was Toure Igan, one of Central's surgical elite, a person to whom only the most delicate geneticomedical problems were posed.

The room they occupied was a tight little space stolen between the walls of an air-system cap servicing the subterranean warrens of the Cascade Complex. Svengaard sat in a comfortable chair, but his arms and legs were bound. Other people were using the space, crowding past the little table where Igan sat. The people carried oddly shaped packages. For the most part they ignored Igan and his companion.

Svengaard studied the dark, intense features of the Central surgeon. Crease lines in the man's face betrayed the beginning of enzymic failure. He was starting to age. But the eyes were the blue of a summer sky and still young.

"You must choose sides," Igan had said.

Svengaard allowed his attention to wander. A man passed carrying a golden metallic ball. From one of his pockets protruded a short silver chain on which dangled a breeder fetish in the shape of a lingam.

"You must answer," Igan said.

Svengaard looked at the wall beside him—plasmeld, the inevitable plasmeld. The space stank of disinfectants and the ersatz-garden effect of air purifier perfumes.

People continued to pass through the narrow room. The sameness of their garments began to weigh on Svengaard. Who were these people? That they were members of the Underground, that was obvious. But *who* were they?

A woman touched him, crowding past. Svengaard looked up into a white smile in a black face, recognized a Zeek female, a face like Potter's but the skin darker . . . a surgical mistake. She wore a bracelet of human hair on her right wrist. It was blonde hair. Svengaard stared at the bracelet until the woman rounded the curve of the room out of his sight.

"It's open battle now," Igan said. "You must believe me. Your own life depends on it."

My own life? Svengaard wondered. He tried to think about his own life, identify it. He had a tertiary wife, little more than a playmate, a woman like himself whose every request for a breeder permit had been denied. For a moment, he couldn't picture her face, lost the shape of it in memories of previous wives and playmates.

She isn't my life, he thought. *Who is my life?*

He was conscious of a fatigue that went to the bone, and a hangover from the narcotics his captors had administered during the night. He remembered the hands seizing him, that gasping look into a wall that could not be a door but was, the lighted space beyond. And he remembered awakening here with Igan across from him.

"I've held nothing back," Igan said. "I've told you everything. Potter barely escaped with his life. The order's already out to get you. Your computer nurse is dead. Many people have died. More will die. They have to be sure, don't you understand? They can leave nothing to chance."

What is my life? Svengaard asked himself. And he thought now about his comfortable apartment, the artifacts and entertainment reels, the reference works, his friends, the safely ordinary routine of his position.

"But where would I go?" Svengaard asked.

"A place has been prepared."

"No place is safe from *them*," Svengaard said. In saying this, he sensed for the first time the depth of his own resentment against the Optimen.

"Many places are safe," Igan said. "*They* merely pretend to supersensual perception. Their real powers lie in machines and instruments, the secret surveillance. But machines and instruments can be twisted to other purposes. And the Optimen depend on Folk to do their violence."

Svengaard shook his head. "This is all nonsense."

"Except for one thing," Igan said, "*they* are as we—variously human. We know this from experience."

"But why would they do these things you accuse them of?" Svengaard protested. "It's not sensible. They're *good* to us."

"Their sole interest is in maintaining themselves," Igan said. "They walk a tightrope. As long as there's no significant change in their environment, they'll continue living . . . indefinitely. Let significant change creep into their lives and they are like us—subject to the whims of nature. For them, you see, there can be no nature—no nature they don't control."

"I don't believe it," Svengaard said. "They're the ones who love us and care for us. Look at all they've done for us."

"I have looked." Igan shook his head. Svengaard was being more pig-headed than they'd expected. He screened out contrary evidence and stuck to the old formulas.

"You want them to succumb," Svengaard accused. "Why do you want this?"

"Because they've deprived us of evolution," Igan said.

Svengaard stared at him. "What?"

"They've made themselves the only free individuals in our world," Igan said. "But individuals don't evolve. Populations evolve, not individuals. We have no population."

"But the Folk—"

"Yes, the Folk! Who among us are allowed to mate?" Igan shook his head. "You're a gene surgeon, man! Haven't you identified the pattern yet?"

"Pattern? What pattern? What do you mean?" Svengaard pushed himself up in the chair, cursed his bindings. His arms and legs felt numb.

"The Optimen hold to one cardinal rule of mating," Igan said. "Return to the standard average. They allow a random interchange with the standard average organism to suppress development of unique individuals. Such few unique individuals as occur are not allowed to breed."

Svengaard shook his head. "I don't believe you," he said. But he could feel the beginnings of doubt. His own case— no matter which mate he chose, the breeding permit was denied. He'd examined the genetic matchings himself, had seen configurations he would've sworn were viable—but the Optimen said no.

"You do believe me," Igan said.

"But look at the long lives they give us," Svengaard said. "I can expect almost two hundred years."

"Medicine does that, not the Optimen," Igan said. "Delicate, careful refinement of the enzymic prescription's the key. That plus a proscribed life in which emotional upset is held to a minimum. Selected exercises and a diet chosen for your specific needs. It could be done for almost anyone."

"Indefinite life?" Svengaard whispered.

"No! But long life, much longer than we get now. I'm going on four hundred years, myself—as are several of my contemporaries. Almost four hundred *lovely* years," he said, remembering Calapine's vicious phrase . . . and Nourse's chuckle.

"Four hundred—you?" Svengaard asked.

"I agree it's nothing compared to *their* many thousands," Igan said. "But almost anyone could have these years, except *they* don't permit it."

"Why?" Svengaard asked.

"This way they can offer the bonus years to the selected few," Igan said, "a reward for service. Without this rule they have no *coin* to buy us. You knew this! You've been trying to sell yourself to them for this coin all your life."

Svengaard looked down at his bound hands. *Is that my life?* he wondered. *Fettered hands? Who will buy my fettered hands?*

"And you should hear Nourse chuckle at my pitiful four hundred years," Igan said.

"Nourse?"

"Yes! Nourse of the Tuyere, Nourse the Cynic, Nourse of the more than forty thousand years! Why do you think Nourse is a Cynic?" Igan demanded. "There're older Optimen, much older. Most of *those* aren't Cynics."

"I don't understand," Svengaard said. He stared at Igan, feeling weak, battered, unable to counter the force of these words and arguments.

"I forget you're not of Central," Igan said. "They classify themselves by the tiny bit of emotion they're permitted. They're Actionists, Emotionals, Cynics, Hedonists and Effetes. They pass through cynicism on their way to hedonism. The Tuyere already's well occupied in pursuit of personal pleasure. There's a pattern here, too, and none of it's good."

Igan studied Svengaard, weighing the effect of his words. Here was a creature barely above the Folk. He was medieval man. To him, Central and the Optimen were the "primum mobile" in control of all celestial systems. Beyond Central lay only the empyrean home of the Creator . . . and for the Svengaards of the world there was little distinction between Optiman and Creator. Both were higher than the moon and totally without fault.

"Where can we run?" Svengaard asked. "There's no place to hide. *They* control the enzymic prescriptions. The minute one of us walks into a pharmacy for renewal, that's the end."

"We have our sources," Igan said.

"But why would you want me?" Svengaard asked. He kept his eyes on his bindings.

"Because you're a unique individual," Igan said. "Because Potter wants you. Because you know of the Durant embryo."

The Durant embryo, Svengaard thought. *What's the significance of the Durant embryo? It all comes back to that embryo.*

He looked up, met Igan's eyes.

"You find it difficult to see the Optimen in my description of them," Igan said.

"Yes."

"They're a plague on the face of the earth," Igan said. "They're the earth's disease!"

Svengaard recoiled from the bitterness of Igan's voice.

"Saul has erased his thousands and David his ten thousands," Igan said. "But the Optimen erase the future."

A blocky hulk of a man squeezed past the narrow space beside the table, planted himself with his back to Svengaard.

"Well?" he asked. The voice carried a disturbing tone of urgency, just in that one word. Svengaard tried to see the face, but couldn't move far enough to the side. There was just that wide belted back in a gray jacket.

"I don't know," Igan said.

"We can spare no more time," the newcomer said. "Potter has completed his work."

"The result?" Igan asked.

"He says successful. He used enzymic injection for quick recovery. The mother will be ready to move soon." A thick hand moved over the shoulder to point a thumb at Svengaard. "What do we do with him?"

"Bring him," Igan said. "What's Central doing?"

"Ordered arrest and confinement of every surgeon."

"So soon? Did they get Dr. Hand?"

"Yes, but he took the black door."

"Stopped his heart," Igan said. "The only thing. We can't let them question one of us. How many does that leave us?"

"Seven."

"Including Svengaard?"

"Eight then."

"We'll keep Svengaard restrained for the time being," Igan said.

"They're beginning to pull their special people out of Seatac," the big man said.

Svengaard could see only half of Igan's face past the newcomer, but that half showed a deep frown of concentration. The one visible eye looked at Svengaard, disregarded him.

"It's obvious," Igan said.

"Yes—they're going to destroy the megalopolis."

"Not destroy, sterilize."

"You've hard Allgood speak of the Folk?"

"Many times. *Vermin in their warrens*. He'll step on the entire region without a qualm. Is everything ready to move?"

"Ready enough."

"The driver?"

"Programed for the desired response."

"Give Svengaard a shot to keep him quiet, then. We won't have time for him once we're on the road."

Svengaard stiffened.

The bulky back turned. Svengaard looked up into a pair of glistening eyes, gray, measuring, devoid of emotion. One of the thick hands lifted, carrying a springshot ampule. The hand touched his neck and there was a jolt.

Svengaard stared up at that faceless face while the fuzzy clouds closed around his mind. His throat felt thick, tongue useless. He willed himself to protest, but no sound came. Awareness became a tightening globe centered on a tiny patch of ceiling with slotted openings. The scene condensed, smaller and smaller—a frantic circle like an eye with slotted pupils.

He sank into a cushioned well of darkness.

13

Lizbeth lay on a bench with Harvey seated beside her, steadying her. There were five people here in a cubed space no bigger than a large packing box. The box had been fitted into the center of a normal load on an overland transporter van. A single glowtube in the corner above her head illuminated the interior with a sickly yellow light. She could see Doctors Igan and Boumour on a rough bench opposite her, their feet stretched across the bound, gagged, and unconscious figure of Svengaard on the floor.

It was already night outside, Harvey had said. That must mean they'd come a goodly distance, she thought. She felt vaguely nauseated and her abdomen ached around the stitches. The thought of carrying her son within her carried a strange reassurance. There was a sense of fulfillment in it. Potter had said she could likely do without her regular enzymes while she carried the embryo. He'd obviously been thinking the embryo would be removed into a vat when they reached a safe place. But she knew she'd resist that. She wanted to carry her son full term. No woman had done that for thousands of years, but she wanted it.

"We're picking up speed," Igan said. "We must be out of the tubes onto the skyway."

"Will there be checkpoints?" Boumour asked.

"Bound to be."

Harvey sensed the accuracy of Igan's assessment. Speed? Yes—their bodies were compensating for heavier pressure on the turns. Air was coming in a bit faster through the scoop ventilator under Lizbeth's bench. There was a new hardness to the ground-effect suspension, less bounce. The turbines echoed loudly in the narrow box and he could smell unburned hydrocarbons.

Checkpoints? Security would use every means to see that no one escaped Seatac. He wondered then what was about to happen to the megalopolis. The surgeons had spoken of poison gas in the ventilators, sonics. Central had many weapons, they said. Harvey put out an arm to hold Lizbeth as they rounded a sharp corner.

He didn't know how he felt about Lizbeth carrying their son within her. It was odd. Not obscene or disgusting . . . just odd. An instinctive response had come to focus within him and he looked around for dangers from which he could protect her. But there was only this box filled with the smell of stale sweat and oil.

"What's the cargo around us?" Boumour asked.

"Odds and ends," Igan said. "Machinery parts, some old art works, inconsequential things. We took anything we could pirate to make a seemingly normal load."

Inconsequentials, Harvey thought. He found himself fascinated by this revelation. Inconsequentials. They carried parts to things that might never be built.

Lizbeth's hand groped out, found his. "Harvey?"

He bent over her. "Yes, dear?"

"I feel . . . so . . . funny."

Harvey cast a despairing look at the doctors.

"She'll be all right," Igan said.

"Harvey, I'm afraid," she said. "We're not going to get through."

"That's no way to talk," Igan said.

She looked up, found the gene surgeon studying her across the narrow space of the box. His eyes were a pair of glittering instruments in a slim, supercilious face. *Is he a Cyborg, too?* she wondered. The cold way the eyes stared at her broke through her control.

"I don't care about myself!" she hissed. "But what about my son?"

"Best calm yourself, madame," Igan said.

"I can't," she said. "We're not going to make it!"

"That's no way to act," Igan said. "Our driver is the finest Cyborg available."

"He'll never get us past *them*," she moaned.

"You'd best be quiet," Igan said.

Harvey at last had an object from which to protect his wife. "Don't talk to her that way!" he barked.

Igan spoke in a long-suffering tone, "Not you, too, Durant. Keep your voice down. You know as well as I do they'll have listening stations along the skyway. We shouldn't be speaking now unless it's absolutely necessary."

"Nothing can get past *them* tonight," Lizbeth whispered.

"Our driver is little more than a shell of flesh around a reflex computer," Igan said. "He's programed for just this task. He'll get us through if anyone can."

"If anyone can," she whispered. She began to sob—wracking, convulsive movements that shook her whole body.

"See what you've done!" Harvey said.

Igan sighed, brought up a hand containing a capsule, extended the capsule to Harvey. "Give her this."

"What's that?" Harvey demanded.

"Just a sedative."

"I don't want a sedative," she sobbed.

"It's for your own good, my dear," Igan said. "Really, this could dislodge the embryo. You should remain calm and quiet this soon after the operation."

"She doesn't want it," Harvey said. His eyes glared with anger.

"She has to take it," Igan said.

"Not if she doesn't want it."

Igan forced his voice into a reasonable tone. "Durant,

I'm only trying to save our lives. You're angry now and you—"

"You're damn' right I'm angry! I'm tired of being ordered around!"

"If I've offended you, I'm sorry, Durant," Igan said. "But I must caution you that your present reaction is conditioned by your gene shaping. You've excess male protectiveness. Your wife will be all right. This sedative is harmless. She's hysterical because she has too much *maternal* drive. These are flaws in your gene shaping, but you'll both be all right if you remain calm."

"Who says we're flawed?" Harvey demanded. "I'll bet you're a Sterrie who's never—"

"That's quite enough, Durant," the other doctor said. It was a rumbling, powerful voice.

Harvey looked at Boumour, noted the pinched-up elfin face on the big body. The surgeon appeared powerful and dangerous, the face strangely inhuman.

"We cannot fight among ourselves," Boumour rumbled. "We may be getting near the checkpoint. They're sure to have listening devices."

"We aren't flawed," Harvey growled.

"Perhaps you're right," Igan said. "But you're both reducing our chances of escape. If one of you breaks up at that checkpoint, that's the end of us." He shifted his hand, extended the capsule to Lizbeth. "Please take this, madam. It contains a tranquilizer. Quite harmless, I assure you."

Hesitantly, Lizbeth took the capsule. It felt cold and gelatinous against her fingers—repulsive. She wanted to hurl the thing at Igan, but Harvey touched her cheek.

"Maybe you'd better take it," he said. "For the baby."

She brought up her hand, popped the capsule against the back of her tongue, gulped it. It must be all right if Harvey agreed. But she didn't like the hurt, baffled look in his eyes.

"Now relax," Igan said. "It's fast acting—three or four minutes and you'll feel quite calm." He sat back, glanced down at Svengaard. The trussed figure still appeared to be unconscious, chest rising and falling in an even rhythm.

For what felt like a long time now, Svengaard had been

increasingly aware of hunger and a swooping, turning motion that rolled his body against a hard surface. There was a sensation of swiftness about the motion. He smelled human perspiration, heard the roar of turbines. The sound was beginning to press on his consciousness. There was light, dim and fuzzy through uncooperative eyelids. He felt a gag biting his lips, bindings on hands and feet.

Svengaard opened his eyes.

For a moment, he failed to focus, then he found himself staring up at a low ceiling, a tiny glowtube in the corner with a speaker grill beneath it bulging beside a dull ruby call light. The ceiling seemed too close to him and there was a blurred shadow shape to his right—a leg stretched across him. The single light emitted a yellow glow that almost failed to dispel the darkness.

The ruby light began winking, red fire flashing on and off, on and off.

"Checkpoint!" Igan hissed. "Silence everyone!"

They sensed the van begin to slow. Its air suspension became softer and softer. The turbines whined downscale. They rocked to a stop and the turbines whispered into standby.

Svengaard's gaze darted around the enclosure. A rough bench above him to his right . . . two figures seated on it. A sharp edge of metal protruded from the bench support beside his cheek. Softly, gently, Svengaard moved his head toward the metal projection, felt it touch flesh through the gag. He gave a gentle push of his head upward and the gag pulled down slightly. The projection scratched his cheek, but he ignored it. Another gentle tug and the gag lowered another fraction of a millimeter. He turned his eyes, checking his surroundings, saw Lizbeth's face above him to the left, her eyes closed, hands in front of her mouth. There was a sense of suspended terror about her.

Again, Svengaard moved his head.

There were voices somewhere in a remote distance—sharp sounds of questions, murmurous answers.

Lizbeth's hands lowered to reveal her mouth. The lips moved soundlessly.

The sound of talking had stopped.

Slowly, the van began to move.

Svengaard twisted his head. The binding of his gag broke free. He coughed it from his mouth, shouted, "Help! Help! I'm a prisoner! Help!"

Igan and Boumour leaped with shock. Lizbeth screamed, "No! Oh, no!"

Harvey surged forward, crashed a fist into Svengaard's jaw, fell on him with one hand over the man's mouth. They held their positions in an agony of listening as the van continued to gather speed.

Igan took a trembling breath, looked across into the wide staring eyes of Lizbeth.

The voice of their driver came through the speaker grill: "What is the trouble? Can't you observe the simplest precautions?"

The dispassionate, accusing quality of the voice chilled Harvey. He wondered about the driver then, why the creature took this tone rather than telling them if they'd been exposed. Svengaard felt limp and unconscious beneath him, Harvey realized. He experienced a wild desire to throttle the surgeon here and now, could almost feel his hands around the man's throat.

"Did they hear us?" Igan whispered.

"Apparently not," the driver rasped. "No sign of pursuit. I presume you'll not permit another such lapse. Please report on what happened."

"Svengaard wakened from the narcotic sooner than we expected."

"But he was gagged."

"He . . . managed to get the gag off, somehow."

"Perhaps you should kill him. Obviously, he will not take reconditioning."

Harvey pushed himself off Svengaard. Now that the Cyborg had made the suggestion, he no longer felt like killing Svengaard. Who was it up there in the van's cab? Harvey wondered. Cyborgs tended to sound alike, that computer personality with its altitude of logic so far above the human.

This one, though, came through even more remote than usual.

"We'll . . . consider what to do," Igan said.

"Svengaard is again secure?"

"He's been taken care of."

"No thanks to you," Harvey said, staring at Igan. "You were right over him."

Igan's faced paled. He remembered his frozen immobility after that leap of fear. Anger surged through him. What right had this clod to question a surgeon? He spoke stiffly, "I regret that I'm not a man of violence."

"Something you'd better learn," Harvey said. He felt Lizbeth's hand on his shoulder, allowed her to guide him back onto their bench. "If you have more of that knock-out stuff, maybe you'd better use another dose of it on him before he wakes up again."

Igan suppressed a sharp reply.

"In the bag under our bench," Boumour said. "A reasonable suggestion."

Woodenly, Igan groped for a slapshot and administered it to Svengaard.

Again, the driver's voice barked through the speaker: "Attention! We must not presume from the lack of immediate and obvious pursuit that they failed to hear the outcry. I am executing Plan Gamma."

"Who is that driver?" Harvey whispered.

"I didn't see which one they programed," Boumour said. He studied Harvey. That had been an appropriate question. The driver did sound odd, much more so than the usual Cyborg abnormality. They'd said the driver would be a programed reflex computer, a machine designed to give the surest response to achieve their escape. Who did they choose for that program?

"What's Plan Gamma?" Lizbeth whispered.

"We're abandoning the prepared escape route," Boumour said. He stared at the forward wall of their box. Abandoning the prepared route . . . which meant they'd be completely dependent now upon the abilities of the Cyborg driver . . . and whichever scattered cells of the Underground remained and were available. Any one of those cells could've been compromised, of course. Boumour's usually stolid nature began to entertain odd wisps of fear.

"Driver!" Harvey called.

"Silence," the driver snapped.

"Stick to the original plan," Harvey said. "They have the medical facilities there if my wife—"

"Your wife's safety is not the overriding factor," the driver said. "Elements along the prepared route must not be discovered. Do not distract me with your objections. Plan Gamma is being executed."

"Easy does it," Boumour said as Harvey surged forward, supporting himself with a hand on the bench. "What can you do, Durant?"

Harvey sagged back onto the bench, groped for and found Lizbeth's hand. She squeezed it, signaled, *"Wait. Don't you read the doctors? They're frightened too . . . and worried."*

"I'm worried about you," Harvey signaled.

So her safety—and presumably ours—aren't the overriding concern, Boumour thought. *What then is the overriding concern? What program controls our computer-in-flesh?*

14

Only Nourse of the Tuyere occupied a throne in the Survey Globe, his attention on the rays, the winking lights and gauges, the cascading luminescences that reported affairs of the Folk. A telltale told him it was night outside in this hemisphere—darkness that spread across the land from Seatac to the megalopolis of N'Scotia. He saw the physical darkness as a sign of frightening events to come and wished Schruille and Calapine would return.

The visual-report screen came alight. Nourse turned to face it as Allgood's features appeared there. The Security boss bowed to Nourse.

"What is it?" Nourse asked.

"Seatac Checkpoint East reports a van with an odd load of containers has just gone through, Nourse. Its turbines carried masking mutes which we deciphered. The mutes concealed sounds of breathing—five persons hidden in the load. Voices cried out from within as the van pulled away. Acting on your instructions, we put a drop marker onto the van and now have it under observation. What are your orders?"

It begins, Nourse thought. *While I'm alone here it begins.*

Nourse looked to the instruments covering the checkpoints. Seatac East. The van was a moving green pinpoint on a screen. He read the banked binaries describing the incident, compared them with a total-plan motivational analysis. The probability analogues he derived filled him with a sense of doom.

"The voices have been identified, Nourse," Allgood said. "The voice prints were—"

"Svengaard and Lizbeth Durant," Nourse said.

"Where she is, her husband cannot be far away," Allgood said.

Allgood's logical little announcements began to annoy Nourse. He contained the emotion while noting the man had overlooked the use of the Optiman's name-in-address. It was a small sign, but significant, especially when Allgood appeared not to notice his own lapse.

"Which leaves us two unidentified," Nourse said.

"We can make an educated guess . . . Nourse."

Nourse glanced at his probability analogues, said, "Two of our wayward pharmacists."

"One may be Potter, Nourse."

Nourse shook his head. "Potter remains in Seatac."

"They may have a portable vat, Nourse, and that embryo with them," Allgood said, "but we failed to detect appropriate machinery."

"You would not hear the machinery being used," Nourse said. "Or, hearing it, you would not identify it."

Nourse looked up to the banks of scanners—every one of them alive—showing the Optimen observing their Survey Globe. Night or day, the watching channels were jammed. *They know what I mean*, he thought. *Are they disgusted, or is this just another interesting aspect of violence?*

As could have been predicted, Allgood said, "I fail to understand Nourse's meaning."

"No need," Nourse said. He looked at the face in the screen. So young it appeared, but Nourse had begun to notice a thing: There was much youngness in Central, but no youth. Even the Sterrie servants betrayed this fact to the unveiled eye. He felt himself to be like the Sterrie Folk suddenly, watching each other for evidence of aging, hoping by comparison that their own appearance prospered.

"What are Nourse's instructions?" Allgood asked.

"Svengaard's outcry indicates he's a prisoner," Nourse said. "But we must not overlook the possibility this is an elaborate ruse." He spoke in a resigned, tired voice.

"Shall we destroy the van, Nourse?"

"Destroy . . ." Nourse shuddered. "No, not yet. Keep it under surveillance. Put out a general alert. We must discover where they're headed. Every contact they make must be noted and marked down for attention."

"If they elude us, Nourse, it could—"

"You've flagtapped the appropriate enzyme prescriptions?"

"Yes, Nourse."

"Then they cannot run far . . . or long."

"As you say, Nourse."

"You may go," Nourse said.

He watched the screen long after it had turned blank. Destroy the van? That would be an ending. He felt then that he did not want this *game* to end—ever. A curious feeling of elation crept through him.

The globe's entrance segment swung open below him. Calapine entered followed by Schruille. They rode the climbing beam to their seats on the triangular dais. Neither spoke. They appeared withdrawn, oddly calm. Nourse, thought of a controlled storm as he looked at them—the lightning and the thunder contained, that it might not harm their fellows.

"Is it not time?" Calapine asked.

A sigh escaped Nourse.

Schruille activated the sensor contact with the scanners in the mountains. There was moonlight suddenly in the receiving screens, the sounds of nightbirds, a rustling of dry leaves. Far off across moon-frosted hills lay lines and patches of lights tracing the coast and harbors of the megalopolis and the multi-level skyway networks.

Calapine stared at the scene, thinking of jewels and casual baubles, the playthings of idleness. She'd not had the inclination in several centuries to indulge in such toys. *Why should I think of them now?* she wondered. *These are not toys, these lights.*

Nourse examined the binary pyramids, the action analogues showing the course of Folk activity within the megalopolis.

"All is normal . . . and in readiness," he said.

"Normal!" Schruille said.

"Which of us?" Calapine whispered.

"I have seen the necessity longest," Schruille said. "I will do it." He rolled a looping ring in the arm of his throne and as he moved it was appalled by the simplicity of the action. This ring and the powers it controlled had been at hand for eons, an insensitive linkage of machinery. All it took was a simple turning motion, a hand and the will behind the hand.

Calapine watched the scene in her screens—moonlight on hills, the megalopolis beyond, an animated toy subject to her whims. The last cadre of special personnel had departed, she knew. Irreplaceable objects that might be damaged had been removed. All was ready and doomed.

Winking flares began to appear through the necklaces of light—golden yellow flares. The Tuyere's screens blurred as sonics vibrated the distant scanners. Lights began going out. Across the entire region, the lights went out—in groups and one by one. A low green fog rolled across the scene, filling in the valleys, overrunning the hills.

Presently, no lights were visible. Only the green fog remained. It continued to creep out beneath the impersonal moon, moving out and across and through until it remained and nothing more.

Schruille watched the stacked numerical analogues, the unemotional reporters which merely counted, submitted deductions of sortings, remainders . . . zeroes. Nothing showed Folk dying in the tubes and warrens, in the streets . . . at their labors . . . at their play.

Nourse sat weeping.

They are dead, all dead, he thought. *Dead.* The word felt peculiar in his mind, devoid of personal meaning. It was a term that could be applied to bacteria perhaps . . . or to weeds. One sterilized an area before bringing in lovely flowers. *Why do I weep?* He tried to remember if he'd ever wept before. *Perhaps there was a time when I wept,* he thought. *But it was so long ago. Ago ... ago ... ago ... time ... time ... wept ... wept.* They were words suddenly without meaning. *That's the trouble with endless life,* he thought. *With too much repetition, everything loses meaning.*

Schruille studied the green fog in his screens. *A few repairs, and we'll be able to send in new Folk,* he thought. *We'll repopulate with Folk of a safer cut.* He wondered then where they'd find the safer Folk. The globe's analysis boards revealed that the Seatac problem was only one of many such pockets. Symptoms were everywhere the same.

He could see the flaw. It centered on the isolation of one generation from another. Lack of traditions and continuity became an obsession with the Folk ... because they seemed to communicate no matter what repressions were tried. Folk sayings would crop up to reveal the deep current beneath.

Schruille quoted to himself: *"When God first created a dissatisfied man, He put that man outside Central."*

But we created these Folk, Schruille thought. *How did we create dissatisfied men?*

He turned then and saw that Calapine and Nourse were weeping.

"Why do you weep?" Schruille demanded.

But they remained silent.

15

Where the last skyway ended, the van took the turn away from the undermountain tube, and held to the wide surface track on the Lester by-way. It led upward through old tunnels to the wilderness reserve and breeder-leave resorts along an almost deserted air-blasted roadbed. There were no slavelights up here, only the moon and the stabbing cyclops beam of the van's headlight.

An occasional omnibus passed them on the down-track, the passenger seats occupied by silent, moody couples, their breeder-leave ended, heading back to the megalopolis. If any of them focused on the van, it was dismissed as a supply carrier for the resorts.

On a banked curve below the Homish Resort Complex, the Cyborg driver made a series of adjustments to his lift controls. Venturis narrowed. Softness went out of the ride. Turbines whined upward to a near destructive keening. The van turned off the roadbed.

Within the narrow box that concealed them, Harvey Durant clutched the bench with one hand and Lizbeth with the other as the van lurched and bounced across the eroded mounds of an ancient railroad right of way, crashed through a screen of alders and turned onto a game track that followed the right of way upward through buck brush and rhododendrons.

"What's happening?" Lizbeth wailed.

The driver's voice rasped through the speaker, "We have left the road. There is nothing to fear."

Nothing to fear, Harvey thought. The idea appeared so ludicrous he had to suppress a chuckle which he realized might be near hysteria.

The driver had turned off all exterior lights and was relying now on the moon and his infra-red vision.

The Cyborg-boosted vision revealed the trail as a snail track through the brush. The van gulped this track for two kilometers, leaving a dusty, leaf-whirling wake to a point where the game trail intersected a forest patrol road—a cleared track matted with dead sallow and bracken from the passage of the patrol vehicles. Here, it turned right like a great hissing prehistoric monster, labored up a hill, roared down the other side and to the top of another hill where it stopped.

Turbines whined down to silence and the van settled onto its skids. The driver emerged, a blocky stub-legged figure with glittering prosthetic arms attached for its present needs. A side panel was ripped off and the Cyborg began unloading cargo, tossing it indiscriminately down through a stand of hemlock into a deep gully.

Within their compartment, Igan lurched to his feet, put his mouth near the speaker-phone, hissed, "Where are we?"

Silence.

"That was stupid," Harvey said. "How do you know why he's stopped?"

Igan ignored the insult. It came after all from a semi-educated dolt. "You can hear him shifting cargo," Igan said. He leaned across Harvey, pounded a palm against the compartment's side. "What's going on out there?"

"Oh, sit down," Harvey said. He put a hand on Igan's chest, pushed. The surgeon stumbled backward onto the opposite bench.

Igan started to bounce back, his face dark, eyes glaring. Boumour restrained him, rumbled, "Serenity, friend Igan."

Igan settled back. Slowly, a look of patience came over his features. "It's odd," he said, "how one's emotions have a way of asserting themselves in spite of—"

"That will pass," Boumour said.

Harvey found Lizbeth's hand, clutched it, signaled, *"Igan's chest—it's convex and hard as plasmeld. I felt it under his jacket."*

"You think he's Cyborg?"

"He breathes normally."

"And he has emotions. I read fear on him."

"Yes . . . but . . ."

"We will be careful."

Boumour said, "You should place more trust in us, Durant. Doctor Igan had deduced that our driver would not be moving cargo unless certain sounds were safe."

"How do we know who's moving cargo?" Harvey asked.

A look of caution fled across Boumour's massive calm. Harvey read it, smiled.

"Harvey!" Lizbeth said. *"You don't think the—"*

"It's our driver out there," Harvey reassured her. *"I can smell the wilderness in the air. There's been no sound of a struggle. One doesn't take a Cyborg without a struggle."*

"But where are we?" she asked.

"In the mountains, the wilderness," Harvey said. *"From the feel of the ride, we're well off the main by-ways."*

Abruptly, their compartment lurched, slid sideways. The single light was extinguished. In the sudden darkness, the wall behind Harvey dropped away. He clutched Lizbeth, whirled, found himself looking out into darkness . . . moonlight . . . their driver a blocky shadow against a distant panorama of the megalopolis with its shimmering networks of light. The moon silvered the tops of trees below them and there was a sharp smell of forest duff, resinous, dank, churned up by the van and not yet settled. The wilderness lay silent as though waiting, analyzing the intrusion.

"Out," the driver said.

The Cyborg turned. Harvey saw the features suddenly illuminated by moonlight, said, "Glisson!"

"Greetings, Durant," Glisson said.

"Why you?" Harvey asked.

"Why not?" Glisson asked. "Get out of there now."

Harvey said: "But my wife isn't—"

"I know about your wife, Durant. She's had plenty of time since the treatment. She can walk if she doesn't exert herself."

Igan spoke at Harvey's ear, "She'll be quite all right. Sit her up gently and help her down."

"I . . . feel all right," Lizbeth said. "Here." She put an arm over Harvey's shoulder. Together, they slid down to the ground.

Igan followed, asked, "Where are we?"

"We are someplace headed for someplace else," Glisson said. "What is the condition of our prisoner?"

Boumour spoke from within the compartment, "He's coming around. Help me lift him out."

"Why've we stopped?" Harvey asked.

"There is steep climbing ahead," Glisson said. "We're dropping the load. A van isn't built for this work."

Boumour and Igan shouldered past them carrying Svengaard, propped him against a stump beside the track.

"Wait here while I disengage the trailer," Glisson said. "You might be considering whether we should abandon Svengaard."

Hearing his name, Svengaard opened his eyes, found himself staring out and down at the distant lights of the megalopolis. His jaw ached where Harvey had struck him and there was a throbbing in his head. He felt hungry, thirsty. His hands were numb beyond the bindings. A dry smell of evergreen needles filled his nostrils. He sneezed.

"Perhaps we *should* get rid of Svengaard," Igan said.

"I think not," Boumour said. "He's a trained man, a possible ally. We're going to need trained men."

Svengaard looked toward the voices. They stood beside the van which was a long silvery shape behind a stubby double cab. A wrenching of metal sounded there. The trailer slid backward on its skids almost two meters before stopping against a mound of dirt.

Glisson returned, squatted beside Svengaard. "What is

our decision?" asked the Cyborg. "Kill him or keep him?"

Harvey gulped, felt Lizbeth clutch his arm.

"Keep him yet awhile," Boumour said.

"If he causes no more trouble," Igan said.

"We could always use his parts," Glisson said. "Or try to grow a new Svengaard and retrain it." The Cyborg stood. "An immediate decision isn't necessary. It is a thing to consider."

Svengaard remained silent, frozen by the emotionless clarity of the man's speech. *A hard, brutal man,* he thought. *A tough man, prepared for any violence. A killer.*

"Into the cab with him then," Glisson said. "Everyone into the cab. We must get . . ." The Cyborg broke off, stared out toward the megalopolis.

Svengaard turned toward the strings of blue-white light glittering far away and cold. A winking golden flare had appeared amidst the lights on his left. Another blazed up beyond it—a giant's bonfire set against the background of distant, moon-frosted mountains. More yellow flares appeared to the right. A bone-chilling rattle of sonics shook him, jarred a sympathetic metal dissonance from the van.

"What's happening?" Lizbeth hissed.

"Quiet!" Glisson said. "Be quiet and observe."

"Gods of life," Lizbeth whispered, "what is it?"

"It is the death of a megalopolis," Boumour said.

Again, sonics rattled the van.

"That hurts," Lizbeth whimpered.

Harvey pulled her close, muttered, "Damn them!"

"Up here it hurts," Igan said, his voice chillingly formal. "Down there it kills."

Green fog began emerging from the wilderness some ten kilometers below them. It rolled out and down like a furious downy sea beneath the moon, engulfing everything—hills, the gem-like lights, the yellow flares.

"Did you think they would use the death fog?" Boumour asked.

"We knew they would use it," Glisson said.

"I suppose so," Boumour said. "Sterilize the area."

"What is it?" Harvey demanded.

"It comes from the vents where they administered the contraceptive gas," Boumour said. "One particle on your skin—the end of you."

Igan moved around, stared down at Svengaard. "They are the ones who love us and care for us," he mocked.

"What's happening?" Svengaard asked.

"Can you not hear?" Igan asked. "Can you not see? Your friends the Optimen are sterilizing Seatac. Did you have friends there?"

"Friends?" There was a broken quality to Svengaard's voice. He turned back to stare at the green fog. The distant lights had all been extinguished.

Again, sonics chattered through them, shook the ground, rattled the van.

"What do you think of *them* now?" Igan asked.

Svengaard shook his head, unable to speak. He wondered why he had no sensory fuse system to shut off this scene. He felt chained to awareness through sense organs gone abnormal beyond any previous experience . . . a permissive aberration. His senses were deceiving him, that was it. This was a special case of self-deception.

"Why don't you answer me?" Igan asked.

"Leave him alone," Harvey said. "We've griefs of our own. Haven't you any feelings?"

"He sees it and does not believe," Igan said.

"How could they?" Lizbeth whispered.

"Self-preservation," Boumour rumbled. "A trait our friend Svengaard doesn't seem to have. Perhaps it was cut out of him."

Svengaard stared at the rolling green cloud. So silent and stealthy it was. The great reach of darkness where once there had been light and life filled him with a raw awareness of his own mortality. He thought of friends down there—the hospital staff—embryos, his playmate-wife.

All destroyed.

Svengaard felt emptied, incapable of any emotion—even grief. He could only question, *What was their purpose?*

"Into the cab with him," Glisson said. "On the floor in the rear."

Ungentle hands lifted Svengaard—he identified Boumour and Glisson. The driver's unemotional quality confused Svengaard. He had never before encountered quite that abstract detachment in a human being.

They pushed him onto the floor of the van's cab. The sharp edge of a seat brace dug into his side. Feet came in around him. Someone put a foot on his stomach, recoiled. The turbines came alive. A door was slammed. They glided into motion.

Svengaard sank into a kind of stupor.

Lizbeth seated above him heaved a deep sigh. Hearing it, Svengaard was roused to a feeling of compassion for her, his first emotion since the shock of seeing the megalopolis die.

Why did they do it? he asked himself. *Why?*

In the darkness, Lizbeth gripped Harvey's hand. She could see in an occasional patch of moonglow the outline of Glisson directly ahead of her. The Cyborg's minimal movement, the sense of power in every action, filled her with growing disquiet. The scar of her operation itched. She wanted to scratch, but feared calling attention to herself. The Courier Service had been a long time building its own organization, deceiving both the Cyborgs and the Optimen. They'd done it partly through self-effacement. Now, in her fear, she sank back into that treatment.

Through their hands, Harvey signaled, *"Boumour and Igan, I read them now. They're new Cyborgs. Probably just a first linkage with implanted computers. They're just learning the price, shedding their normal human emotional reactions, learning to counterfeit emotion."*

She absorbed this, seeing them through Harvey's deduction. He often read people better than she did. She reread what she had seen of the two surgeons.

"Do you read it?" he signaled.

"You're right. Yes."

"It means a total break with Central. They can never go back."

"That explains Seatac," she signaled. She began to tremble.

"And we can't trust them," Harvey said. He pressed her close, soothing her.

The van labored up through the foothills skirting open meadows, following ancient tracks, an occasional stream-bed. Shortly before dawn, it swerved left down a fire-break and into a stand of pines and cedars, squeezed its way through a narrow lane there with its blowers kicking up a heavy cloud of forest duff behind. Glisson pulled to a stop behind an old building, moss on its sides, small cur-tained windows. Pseudo-ducks with a weedy patina and grass-grown signs that they hadn't been animated in years, made a short file near the building—pale moon-figures—in the light of a single bulb high up under the building's eaves.

Turbines whined to silence. They could hear then the hum of machinery and looking toward the sound saw the dull silver outline of a ventilator tower among the trees.

A door at the corner of the building opened. A heavy headed man with a big jaw, stoop-shouldered, emerged blowing his nose into a red handkerchief. He looked old, his face a mask of subservience.

Glisson said, "It's the sign. All is safe here . . . for the moment." He slipped out, approached the old man, coughed.

"A lot of sickness around these days," the old man said. His voice was as ancient as his face, wheezing, slurring the consonants.

"You're not the only one with troubles," Glisson said.

The old man straightened, shed the stooped look and subservient manner. "S'pose you're wanting a hidey hole," he said. "Don't know if it's safe here. Don't even know if I oughta hide you."

"I will give the orders here," Glisson said. "You will obey."

The old man studied Glisson a moment, then a look of anger washed over his face. "You damn' Cyborgs!" he said.

"Hold your tongue," Glisson said, his voice flat. "We need food, a safe place to spend the day. I shall require your help in hiding this van. You must know the surrounding terrain. And you will arrange other transportation for us."

"Best cut it up and bury it," the old man said, his voice surly. "Been a hornet's nest stirred up. Guess you know that."

"We know," Glisson said. He turned, beckoned to the van. "Come along. Bring Svengaard."

Presently, the others joined him. Boumour and Igan supported Svengaard between them. The bindings on Svengaard's feet had been released, but he appeared barely able to stand. Lizbeth walked with the bent-over care that said she wasn't sure her incision had healed despite the enzymic speed-up medication.

"We will lodge here during daylight," Glisson said. "This man will direct you to quarters."

"What word from Seatac?" Igan asked.

Glisson looked at the old man, said, "Answer."

The oldster shrugged. "Courier through here couple of hours ago. Said no survivors."

"Any report on a Dr. Potter?" Svengaard croaked.

Glisson whirled, stared at Svengaard.

"Dunno," the old man said. "What route he take?"

Igan cleared his throat, glanced at Glisson, then at the old man. "Potter? I believe he was in the group coming out by the power tubes."

The old man flicked a glance at the ventilator tower growing more distinct among the trees by the second as daylight crept across the mountains. "Nobody come through the tubes," he said. "They shut off the ventilators and flooded the tubes with that gas first thing." He looked at Igan. "Ventilators been going again for about three hours."

Glisson studied Svengaard, asked, "Why are you interested in Potter?"

Svengaard remained silent.

"Answer me!" Glisson ordered.

Svengaard tried to swallow. His throat ached. He felt driven into a corner. Glisson's words enraged him. Without warning, Svengaard lurched forward dragging Igan and Boumour, lashed out at Glisson with a foot.

The Cyborg dodged with a blurring movement, caught the foot, jerked Svengaard from the two surgeons, whirled, swung Svengaard wide and released him. Svengaard landed on his back, skidded across the ground, stopped. Before he could move, Glisson was standing over him. Svengaard lay there sobbing.

"Why are you interested in Potter?" Glisson demanded.

"Go away, go away, go away!" Svengaard sobbed.

Glisson straightened, looked around at Igan and Boumour. "You understand this?"

Igan shrugged. "It's emotion."

"Perhaps a shock reaction," Boumour said.

Through their hands, Harvey signaled Lizbeth, *"He's been in shock, but this mean's he's coming out of it. These are medical people! Can't they read anything?"*

"Glisson reads it," she answered. *"He was testing them."*

Glisson turned around, looked squarely at Harvey. The bold understanding in the Cyborg's eyes shot a pang of fear through Harvey.

"Careful," Lizbeth signaled. *"He's suspicious of us."*

"Take Svengaard inside," Glisson said.

Svengaard looked up at their driver. Glisson, the Durants called him. But the old man from the building had labeled Glisson a Cyborg. Was it possible? Were the half-men being revived to challenge the Optimen once more? Was that the reason for Seatac's death?

Boumour and Igan lifted him, checked the fetters on his hands. "Let's have no more foolishness," Boumour said.

Are they like Glisson? Svengaard asked himself. *Are they, too, part man, part machine? And what about the Durants?*

Svengaard could feel the tear dampness in his eyes. *Hysteria*, he thought. *Coming out of shock.* He began to wonder at himself then with an odd feeling of guilt. Why does Potter's death strike me more deeply than the death of an

entire megalopolis, the extinction of my wife and friends?
What did Potter symbolize to me?

Boumour and Igan half carried, half walked him into the
building, down a narrow hall and into a poorly lighted,
gloomy big room with a ceiling that went up to bare beams
two stories above. They dropped him onto a dusty couch—
bare plastic and hydraulic contour-shapers that adjusted re-
luctantly. The light came from two glowglobes high up under the beams. It exposed oddments of furniture scattered
around the room and mounds of strange shapes covered by
slick, glistening fabric. A table to his left, he realized, was
made of planks. Wood! A contour cot lay beyond it, and
an ancient roll-top desk with a missing drawer, and mis-
matched chairs. A stained, soot-blackened fireplace, with
an iron crane reaching across its mouth like a gibbet, occupied half the wall across from him. The entire room
smelled of dampness and rot. The floor creaked as people
moved. Wood flooring!

Svengaard looked up at tiny windows admitting a sparse
gray daylight that grew brighter by the second. Even at its
brightest he knew it wouldn't dispel the gloom of this place.
Here was sadness that made him think of people without
number—dead, forgotten. Tears rolled down his cheeks.

What's wrong with me? he wondered.

There came a sound from the yard of the van's turbines
being ignited. He heard it lift, leave . . . fade away. Harvey
and Lizbeth entered the room.

Lizbeth looked at Svengaard, then at Boumour and Igan
who had taken up vigil on the cot. With her crouched, pro-
tective walk, she crossed to Svengaard, touched his shoulder. She saw his tears, evidence of humanity, and she
wished then that he were her doctor. Perhaps there was a
way. She decided to ask Harvey.

"Please trust us," she said. "We won't harm you. *They*
are the ones who killed your wife and friends, not us."

Svengaard pulled away.

How dare she have pity on me? he thought. But she had
reached some chord in him. He could feel himself shatter-
ing.

Oppressive silence settled over the room.

Harvey came up, guided his wife to a chair at the table.

"It's wood," she said, touching the surface, wonder in her voice. Then, "Harvey, I'm very hungry."

"They'll bring food as soon as they've disposed of the van," he said.

She clutched his hand and Svengaard watched, fascinated by the nervous movement of her fingers.

Glisson and the old man returned presently, slamming the door behind them. The building creaked with their movement.

"We'll have a forest patrol vehicle for the next stage," Glisson said. "Much safer. There's a thing you all should know now." The Cyborg moved a cold, weighted stare from face to face. "There was a marker on top of the van's load section which we abandoned last night."

"Marker?" Lizbeth said.

"A device for tracing us, following us," Glisson said.

"Ohhh!" Lizbeth put a hand over her mouth.

"I do not know how closely they were following," Glisson said. "I was altered for this task and certain of my devices were left behind. They may know where we are right now."

Harvey shook his head. "But why . . . ?"

"Why haven't they moved against us?" Glisson asked. "It's obvious. They hope we'll lead them to the vitals of our organization." Something like rage came into the Cyborg's features. "It may be we can surprise them."

16

I n the Survey Room, the great globe's instrumented inner
walls lay relatively quiescent. Calapine and Schruille of
the Tuyere occupied the triple thrones. The dais turned
slowly, allowing them to scan the entire surface. Kaleidoscopic colors from the instruments played a somnolent visible melody across Calapine's features—a wash of greens,
reds, purples.

She felt tired with a definite emotion of self-pity. There
was something wrong with the enzymic analyzers. She felt
sure of it, wondering if the Underground had somehow
compromised the function of the pharmacy computers.

Schruille was no help. He'd laughed at the suggestion.

Allgood's features appeared on a call screen before Calapine. She stopped the turning dais as he bowed, said, "I
call to report, Calapine." She noted the dark circles under
his eyes, the drugged awareness in the way he held his head
stiffly erect.

"You have found them?" Calapine asked.

"They're somewhere in the wilderness area, Calapine,"
Allgood said. "They have to be in there."

"Have to be!" she sneered. "You're a foolish optimist,
Max."

"We know some of the hiding places they could've chosen, Calapine."

"For every one you know, they've nine you don't know," she said.

"I have the entire area ringed, Calapine. We're moving in slowly, checking everywhere as we go. They're there and we'll find them."

"He babbles," she said, glancing at Schruille.

Schruille returned a mirthless smile, looked at Allgood through the prismatic reflector. "Max, have you found the source of the substitute embryo?"

"Not yet, Schruille."

He stared up at them, his face betraying his obvious confusion at the militancy and violence of *his* Optimen.

"Do you seek in Seatac?" Calapine demanded.

Allgood wet his lips with his tongue.

"Out with it!" she snapped. *Ahhh, the fear in his eyes.*

"We're searching there, Calapine, but the—"

"You think we were too precipitate?" she asked.

He shook his head.

"You're acting strangely," Schruille said. "Are you afraid of us?"

He hesitated, then, "Yes, Schruille."

"Yes, Schruille!" Calapine mimicked.

Allgood looked at her, the fear in his eyes tempered by anger. "I'm taking every action I know, Calapine."

She marked a sudden precision in his manner behind the anger. Her eyes went wide with wonder. Was it possible? She looked at Schruille, wondering if he had seen it.

"Max, why did you call us?" Schruille asked.

"I . . . to report, Schruille."

"You've reported nothing."

Hesitantly, Calapine brought up her instruments for a special probe of Allgood, stared at the result. Horror mingled with rage in her. Cyborg! They had defiled Max! Her Max!

"There's only need for you to obey us," Schruille said.

Allgood nodded, remained silent.

"You!" Calapine hissed. She leaned toward the screen. "You dared! Why? Why, Max?"

Schruille said, "What . . . ?"

But in the shocked instant of her questions, Allgood had seen that he was discovered. He knew it was his end, could see it in her eyes. "I saw . . . I found the dopplegangers," he stammered.

An angry twist of her hand rolled one of the rings on her throne arm. Sonics sent a shock wave chattering across Allgood, blurred his image. His lips moved soundlessly, eyes staring. He collapsed.

"Why did you do that?" Schruille asked.

"He was Cyborg!" she grated, and pointed to the evidence of the instruments.

"Max? Our Max?" He looked at the instruments, nodded.

"*My* Max," she said.

"But he worshipped you, loved you."

"He does nothing now," she whispered. She blanked the screen, continued to stare at it. Already, the incident was receding from her mind.

"Do you enjoy direct action?" Schruille asked.

She met his gaze in the reflector. *Enjoy direct action? There was indeed a kind of elation in . . . violence.*

"We have no Max now," Schruille said.

"We'll waken another doppleganger," she said. "Security can function without him for now."

"Who'll waken the doppleganger?" Schruille asked. "Igan and Boumour are no longer with us. The pharmacist, Hand, is gone."

"What's keeping Nourse?" she asked.

"Enzymic trouble," Schruille said, a note of glee in his voice. "He said something about a necessary realignment of his prescription. Bonellia hormone derivatives, I believe."

"Nourse can awaken the doppleganger," she said. She wondered momentarily then why they needed the doppleganger. Oh, yes. Max was gone.

"There's more to it than merely awakening Max's duplicate," Schruille said. "They're not as good as they once were, you know. The new Max must be educated for his role, fitted into it gently. It could be weeks . . . months."

"Then one of us can run Security," she said.

"You think we're ready for it?" Schruille asked.

"There's a *thrill* in this sort of decision-making," she said. "I don't mind saying I've been deeply bored during the past several hundred years. But now—now, I feel alive, vital, alert, fascinated." She looked up at the glowing banks of scanner eyes, a full band of them, showing their fellow Optimen watching activities in the Survey Room. "And I'm not alone in this."

Schruille glanced up at the glittering arctic circle of the globe's inner wall. "Aliveness," he murmured. "But Max . . . he is dead."

She remembered then, said, "Any Max can be replaced." She looked at Schruille, turning her head to stare past the prism. "You're very blunt today, Schruille. You've spoken of death twice that I recall."

"Blunt? I?" He shook his head. "But I didn't *erase* Max."

She laughed aloud. "My own reactions thrill me, Schruille!"

"And do you find changes in your enzymic demands?"

"A few. What is that? Times change. It's part of being. Adjustments must be made."

"Indeed," he said.

"Where'd they find a substitute for the Durant embryo?" she asked, her mind shooting off at a tangent.

"Perhaps the new Max can discover," Schruille said.

"He must."

"Or you will grow another Max?" Schruille said.

"Don't mock me, Schruille."

"I wouldn't dare."

Again, she looked directly at him.

"What if they produced their own embryo for the substitution?" Schruille asked.

She turned away. "In the name of all that's proper, how?"

"Air can be filtered clean of contraceptive gas," Schruille said.

"You're disgusting!"

"Am I? But haven't you wondered what Potter concealed?"

"Potter? We know what he concealed."

"A person devoted to the preservation of life . . . such as that is," Schruille said. "What did he hide in his mind?"

"Potter is no more."

"But what did he conceal?"

"You think he knew the source of the . . . outside interference?"

"Perhaps. And *he* would know where to find an embryo."

"Then the record will show the source, as you said yourself."

"I've been reconsidering."

She stared at him in the prism. "It's not possible."

"That I could reconsider?"

"You know what I mean—what you're thinking."

"But it *is possible*."

"It isn't!"

"You're being stubborn, Cal. A female should be the last person to deny such a possibility."

"Now, you're being truly disgusting!"

"We know Potter found a self-viable," Schruille pressed. "They could have many self-viables—male and female. We know historically the capabilities of such raw union. It's part of our *natural* ancestry."

"You're unspeakable," she breathed.

"You can face the concept of death but not this," Schruille said. "Most interesting."

"Disgusting!" she barked.

"But possible," Schruille said.

"The substitute embryo wasn't self-viable!" she pounced.

"All the more reason they might've been willing to sacrifice it for one that was, eh?"

"Where would they find the vat facilities, the chemicals, the enzymes, the—"

"Where they've always been."

"What?"

"They've put the Durant embryo back into its mother,"

Schruille said. "We can be certain of this. Would it not be equally logical to leave the embryo there to begin with—never remove it, never isolate the gametes in a vat at all?"

Calapine found herself speechless. She sensed a sour taste in her mouth, realized with a feeling of shock that she wanted to vomit. *Something's wrong with my enzyme balance,* she thought.

She spoke slowly, precisely, "I am reporting to pharmacy at once, Schruille. I do not feel well."

"By all means," Schruille said. He glanced up and around at the watching scanners—a full circle of them.

Delicately, Calapine eased herself out of her throne, slid down the beam to the lock segment. Before letting herself out, she cast a look up at the dais, faintly remembering. *Which Max was . . . erased?* she asked herself. *We've had many of him . . . a successful model for our Security.* She thought of the others, Max after Max after Max, each shunted aside when his appearance began to annoy his masters. They stretched into infinity, images in an endless system of mirrors.

What is erasure to such as Max? she wondered. *I am an unbroken continuity of existence. But a doppleganger doesn't remember. A doppleganger breaks the continuity.*

Unless the cells remember.

Memory . . . cells . . . embryos . . .

She thought of the embryo within Lizbeth Durant. Disgusting, but simple. So beautifully simple. Her gorge began to rise. Whirling, Calapine dropped down to the Hall of Counsel, ran for the nearest pharmacy outlet. As she ran, she clenched the hand that had slain Max and helped destroy a megalopolis.

17

S he's sick, I tell you!"
Harvey bent over Igan shaking him out of sleep.
They were in a narrow earth-walled room, ceiling of plasmeld beams, a dim yellow glowglobe in one corner. Sleep-
ing pads were spread against the walls, Boumour and Igan
on two of them foot to foot, the bound form of Svengaard
on another, two of the pads empty.

"Come quickly!" Harvey pleaded. "She's sick."

Igan groaned, sat up. He glanced at his watch—almost
sunset on the surface. They'd crawled in here just before
daylight and after a night of laboring on foot up seemingly
endless woods trails behind a Forest Patrol guide. Igan still
ached from the unaccustomed exercise.

Lizbeth sick?

She'd had three days since the embryo had been placed
within her. The others had healed this rapidly, but they
hadn't been subject to a night of stumbling along rough
forest trails.

"Please hurry," Harvey pleaded.

"I'm coming," Igan said. And he thought, *Listen to his
tone change now that he needs me.*

Boumour sat up opposite him, asked, "Shall I join you?"

"Wait here for Glisson," Igan said.

"Did Glisson say where he was going?"

"To arrange for another guide. It'll be dark soon."

"Doesn't he ever sleep?" Boumour asked.

"Please!" Harvey begged.

"Yes!" Igan snapped. "What're her symptoms?"

"Vomiting . . . incoherent."

"Let me get my bag." Igan retrieved a thick black case from the floor near his head, glanced across at Svengaard. The man's breathing still showed the even rhythm of the narcotic they'd administered before collapsing into sleep themselves. Something had to be done about Svengaard. He slowed them down.

Harvey pulled at Igan's sleeve.

"I'm coming! I'm coming!" Igan said. He freed his arm, followed Harvey through a low hole at the end of the room and into a room similar to the one they'd just vacated. Lizbeth lay on a pad beneath a single glowglobe across from them. She groaned.

Harvey knelt beside her. "I'm right here."

"Harvey," she whispered. "Oh, Harvey."

Igan joined them, lifted a pulmonometer-sphagnomometer from his bag. He pressed it against her neck, read the dial. "Where do you hurt?" he asked.

"Ohhhh," she moaned.

"Please," Harvey said, looking at Igan. "Please do something."

"Stand out of the way," Igan said.

Harvey stood up, backed off two steps. "What is it?" he whispered.

Igan ignored him, taped an enzymic vampire gauge to Lizbeth's left wrist, read the dials.

"What's wrong with her?" Harvey demanded.

Igan unclipped his instruments, restored them to his bag. "Nothing's wrong with her."

"But she's—"

"She's perfectly normal. Most of the others reacted the same way. It's realignment of her enzymic demand system."

"Isn't there some—"

"Calm down!" Igan stood up, faced Harvey. "She barely needs any prescription material. Pretty soon, she can do without altogether. She's in better health than you are. And she could walk into a pharmacy right now. The prescription flag wouldn't even identify her."

"Then why's she . . . ?

"It's the embryo. It compensates for her needs to protect itself. Does it automatically."

"But she's sick!"

"A bit of glandular maladjustment, nothing else." Igan picked up his bag. "It's all part of the ancient process. The embryo says produce this, produce that. She produces. Puts a certain strain on her system."

"Can't you do anything for her?"

"Of course I can. She'll be extremely hungry in a little while. We'll give her something to settle her stomach and then feed her. Provided they can produce some food in this hole."

Lizbeth groaned, "Harvey?"

He knelt beside her, clasped her hands. "Yes, dear?"

"I feel terrible."

"They'll give you something in a few minutes."

"Ohhhhh."

Harvey turned a fierce scowl up at Igan.

"As soon as we can," Igan said. "Don't worry. This is normal." He turned, ducked out into the other room.

"What's wrong?" Lizbeth whispered.

"It's the embryo," Harvey said. "Didn't you hear?"

"Yes. My head aches."

Igan returned with a capsule and a cup of water, bent over Lizbeth. "Take this. It'll settle your stomach."

Harvey helped her sit up, held her while she swallowed the capsule.

She took a quavering breath, returned the cup. "I'm sorry to be such a—"

"Quite all right," Igan said. He looked at Harvey. "Best bring her in the other room. Glisson will return in a few minutes. He should have food and a guide."

Harvey helped his wife to her feet, supported her as they

followed Igan into the other room. They found Svengaard sitting up staring at his bound hands.

"Have you been listening?" Igan asked.

Svengaard looked at Lizbeth. "Yes."

"Have you thought about Seatac?"

"I've thought."

"You're not thinking of releasing him," Harvey said.

"He slows us too much," Igan said. "And we *cannot* release him."

"Then perhaps I should do something about him," Harvey said.

"What do you suggest, Durant?" Boumour asked.

"He's a danger to us," Harvey said.

"Ahh," Boumour said. "Then we leave him to you."

"Harvey!" Lizbeth said. She wondered if he'd suddenly gone mad. Was this his reaction to her request that they seek Svengaard as her doctor?

But Harvey was remembering Lizbeth's moans. "If it's him or my son," he said, "the choice is easy."

Lizbeth took his hand, signaled, *"What're you doing? You can't mean this!"*

"What is he, anyway?" Harvey asked, staring at Igan. And he signaled Lizbeth, *"Wait. Watch."*

She read her husband then, pulled away.

"He's a gene surgeon," Harvey said. His voice dripped scorn. "He's existed for *them.* Can he justify his existence? He's a nonviable, nonliving nonentity. He has no future."

"Is that your choice?" Boumour asked.

Svengaard looked up at Harvey. "Do you talk of murdering me?" he asked. The lack of emotion in his voice surprised Harvey.

"You don't protest?" he asked.

Svengaard tried to swallow. His throat felt full of dry cotton. He looked at Harvey, measuring the bulk of the man, the corded muscles. He remembered the excessive male protectiveness in Harvey's nature, the gene-error that made him a slave to Lizbeth's slightest need.

"Why should I argue," Svengaard asked, "when much of

what he says is true and when he's already made up his mind?"

"How will you do it, Durant?" Boumour asked.

"How would you like me to do it?" Harvey asked.

"Strangulation might be interesting," Boumour said, and Harvey wondered if Svengaard, too, could hear the Cyborg clinical detachment in the man's voice.

"A simple snap of the neck is quicker," Igan said. "Or an injection. I could supply several from my kit."

Harvey felt Lizbeth trembling against him. He patted her arm, disengaged himself.

"Harvey!" she said.

He shook his head, advanced on Svengaard.

Igan retreated to Boumour's side, stood watching.

Harvey knelt behind Svengaard, closed his fingers around the surgeon's throat, bent close to the ear opposite his audience. In a whisper audible only to Svengaard, Harvey said, "They would as soon see you dead. They don't care one way or another. How do you feel about it?"

Svengaard felt the hands on his throat. He knew he could reach up with his bound hands and try to remove those clutching fingers, but he knew he'd fail. There was no doubting Harvey's strength.

"Your own choice?" Harvey whispered.

"Do it, man!" Boumour called.

Only seconds ago, Svengaard realized, he'd been resigned to death, wanted death. Suddenly, that wish was the farthest thing from his desires.

"I want to live," he husked.

"Is that your choice?" Harvey whispered.

"Yes!"

"Are you talking to him?" Boumour asked.

"Why do you want to live?" Harvey asked in a normal voice. He relaxed his fingers lightly, a subtle communication to Svengaard. Even an untrained person could *read* this.

"Because I've never *been* alive," Svengaard said. "I want to try it."

"But how can you justify your existence?" Harvey asked,

and he allowed his fingers to tighten ever so slightly.

Svengaard looked at Lizbeth, sensing at last the direction of Harvey's thoughts. He glanced at Boumour and Igan.

"You haven't answered my question," Boumour said. "What are you discussing with our prisoner?"

"Are they both Cyborgs?" Svengaard asked.

"Irretrievably," Harvey said. "Without human feelings— or near enough to it that it makes no difference."

"Then how can you trust them with you wife's care?"

Harvey's fingers relaxed.

"That is a way I could justify my existence," Svengaard said.

Harvey removed his hands from Svengaard's throat, squeezed the man's shoulders. It was instant communication, more than words, something that went from flesh to flesh. Svengaard knew he had an ally.

Boumour crossed to stand over them, demanded, "Are you going to kill him or aren't you?"

"No one here's going to kill him," Harvey said.

"Then what've you been doing?"

"Solving a problem," Harvey said. He kept a hand on Svengaard's arm. Svengaard found he could understand Harvey's intent just by the pressure of that hand. It said, *"Wait. Be still. Let me handle this."*

"And what is your intention now toward our prisoner?" Boumour demanded.

"I intend to free him and put my wife in his care," Harvey said.

Boumour glared at him. "And if that incurs our displeasure?"

"What idiocy!" Igan blared. "How can you trust *him* when we're available?"

"This is a fellow human," Harvey said. "What he does for my wife will be out of humanity and not like a mechanic treating her as a machine for transporting an embryo."

"This is nonsense!" Igan snapped. But he realized then that Harvey had recognized their Cyborg nature.

Boumour raised a hand to silence him as Igan started to

continue talking. "You have not indicated how you will do this if we oppose it," he said.

"You're not full Cyborgs," Harvey said. "I see in you fears and uncertainties. It's new to you and you're changing. I suspect you're very vulnerable yet."

Boumour backed off three steps, his eyes measuring Harvey. "And Glisson?" Boumour asked.

"Glisson wants only trustworthy allies," Harvey said. "I'm giving him a trustworthy ally."

"How do you know you can trust Svengaard?" Igan demanded.

"Because you have to ask, you betray your ineffectiveness," Harvey said. He turned, began unfastening Svengaard's fetters.

"It's on your head," Boumour said.

Harvey freed Svengaard's hands, knelt and removed the bindings from his feet.

"I'm going for Glisson," Igan said. He left the room.

Harvey stood up, faced Svengaard. "Do you know about my wife's condition?" he asked.

"I heard Igan," Svengaard said. "Every surgeon studies history and genetic origins. I have an academic knowledge of her condition."

Boumour sniffed.

"There's Igan's medical kit," Harvey said, pointing to the black case on the floor. "Tell me why my wife was sick."

"You're not satisfied with Igan's explanation?" Boumour asked. He appeared outraged by the thought.

"He said it was natural," Harvey said. "How can sickness be natural?"

"She has received medication," Svengaard said. "Do you know what it was?"

"It had the same markings as the pill he gave her in the van," Harvey said. "A tranquilizer he called it then."

Svengaard approached Lizbeth, looked at her eyes, her skin. "Bring the kit," he said, nodding to Harvey. He guided Lizbeth to an empty pad, finding himself fascinated by the idea of this examination. Once he had thought of this as disgusting; now, the idea that Lizbeth carried an embryo in her in the ancient way held only mystery for him, a profound curiosity.

Lizbeth sent a questioning look at Harvey as Svengaard eased her back onto the pad. Harvey nodded reassuringly. She tried to smile, but a strange fear had come over her. The fear didn't originate with Svengaard. His hands were full of gentle assurance. But the prospect of being examined frightened her. She could feel terror warring with the drug Igan had given her.

Svengaard opened the kit, remembering the diagrams and explanations from the study tapes of his school years. They had been the subject of ribald jokes then, but even the jokes helped him now because they tended to fix vital facts in his mind.

> Cling to the wall, for if you fall,
> You then must learn to do the crawl!

In his memory, he could hear the chant and the uproarious burst of laughter.

Svengaard bent to his examination, excluding all else but the patient and himself. Blood pressure . . . enzymes . . . hormone production . . . bodily secretions . . .

Presently, he sat back, frowned.

"Is something wrong?" Harvey asked.

Boumour stood, arms folded, behind Harvey. "Yes, do tell us," he said.

"Menstrual hormone complex is much too high," Svengaard said. And he thought, *"Cling to the wall . . ."*

"The embryo controls these changes," Boumour sneered.

"Yes," Svengaard said. "But why this shift in hormone production?"

"From your superior knowledge, you'll now tell us," Boumour said.

Svengaard ignored the mocking tone, looked up at Boumour. "You've done this before. Have you had any spontaneous abortions in your patients?"

Boumour frowned.

"Well?" Svengaard said.

"A few." He supplied the information grudgingly.

"I suspect the embryo isn't firmly attached to the endometrium," Svengaard said. "To the wall of the uterus," he said, recognizing Harvey's need for explanation. "The embryo must cling to the uterus wall. The way of this is prepared by hormones present during the menstrual cycle."

Boumour shrugged. "Well, we expect to loose a certain percentage."

"My wife is not a *certain percentage*," Harvey growled. He turned, focused a glare on Boumour that sent the man retreating three steps.

"But these things happen," Boumour said. He looked at Svengaard, who was preparing a slapshot ampule from Igan's kit. "What're you doing?"

"Giving her a little enzymic stimulation to produce the hormones she needs," Svengaard said. He glanced at Harvey, seeing the man's fears and need for reassurance. "It's the best thing we can do now, Durant. It should work if her system hasn't been too upset by all this." He waved a hand indicating their flight, the emotional stress, the exertion.

"Do whatever you think you should," Harvey said. "I know it's your best."

Svengaard administered the shot, patted Lizbeth's arm. "Try to rest. Relax. Don't move around unless it's necessary."

Lizbeth nodded. She had been reading Svengaard, seeing his genuine concern for her. His attempt to reassure Harvey had touched her, but there were fears she couldn't suppress.

"Glisson," she whispered.

Svengaard saw the direction of her thoughts, and said, "I won't permit him to move you until I'm sure you're all right. He and his guide will just have to wait."

"*You* won't permit!" Boumour sneered.

As though to punctuate his words, the ground around them rumbled and shook. Dust puffed through the low entrance and, like a magician's trick, Glisson materialized there as the concealing dust settled.

At the first sign of disturbance, Harvey had dropped to the floor beside Lizbeth. He held her shoulders, shielded her with his body.

Svengaard still knelt beside the medical kit.

Boumour had whirled to stare at Glisson. "Sonics?" Boumour hissed.

"Not sonics," Glisson said. The Cyborg's usually flat voice carried a sing-song twang.

"He has no arms," Harvey said.

They all noticed it then. From the shoulders down where Glisson's arms had been now dangled only the empty linkages for Cyborg prosthetic attachments.

"*They* have sealed us in here," Glisson said. Again, that sing-song twang as though something about him had been broken. "As you can see, I am disarmed. Do you not think that amusing? Do you see now why we could never fight *them* openly? When they wish it, they can destroy anything . . . anyone."

"Igan?" Boumour whispered.

"Igans are easy to destroy," Glisson said. "I have seen it. Accept the fact."

"But what'll we do?" Harvey demanded.

"Do?" Glisson looked down at him. "We will wait."

"One of you could stand off an entire Security force to get Potter away," Boumour said. "But all you can do now is wait?"

"Violence is not my function," Glisson said. "You will see."

"What'll they do?" Lizbeth hissed.

"Whatever they wish to do," Glisson said.

18

T here, it is done," Calapine said.
    She looked at Schruille and Nourse in the reflectors.
    Schruille indicated the kinesthetic analogue relays of the
Survey Globe's inner wall. "Did you observe Svengaard's
emotion?"

"He was properly horrified," Calapine said.

Schruille pursed his lips, studied her reflection. A session
with the pharmacy had restored her composure, but she
occupied her throne in a subdued mood. The kaleidoscopic
play of lights from the wall gave an unhealthy cast to her
skin. There was a definite flush to her features.

Nourse glanced up at the observer lights—the span of
arctic wall glowed with a dull red intensity, every position
occupied. With hardly an exception, the Optiman community watched developments.

"We have a decision to make," Nourse said.

"You look pale, Nourse," Calapine said. "Did you have
pharmacy trouble?"

"No more than you." He spoke defensively. "A simple
enzymic heterodyning. It's pretty well damped out."

"I say bring them here now," Schruille said.

"To what purpose?" Nourse asked. "We have the pattern
of their flight very well fixed. Why let them escape again?"

"I don't like the thought of unregistered self-viables—who knows how many—running loose out there," Schruille said.

"Are you sure we could take them alive?" Calapine asked.

"The Cyborg admits ineffectiveness against us," Schruille said.

"Unless that's a trick," Nourse said.

"I don't think so," Calapine said. "And once we have them here we can extract the information we need from their raw brains with the utmost precision."

Nouse turned, stared at her. He couldn't understand what had happened to Calapine. She spoke with the callous brutality of a Folk woman. She was like an awakened ghoul, as though violence were her rising bell.

What is her setting bell? he wondered. And he was shocked at his own thought.

"If they have means of destroying themselves?" Nourse asked. "I remind you of the computer nurse and a sad number of our own surgeons who appear to be in league with these criminals. We were powerless to prevent their self-destruction."

"How callous you are, Nourse," Calapine said.

"Callous? I?" He shook his head. "I merely wish to prevent further pain. Let us destroy them ourselves and go on from here."

"Glisson's a full Cyborg," Schruille said. "Can you imagine what his memory banks would reveal?"

"I remember the one who escorted Potter," Nourse said. "Let us take no risk. His quietude could be a trick."

"A contact narcotic in their present cell," Schruille said. "That's my suggestion."

"How do you know it'll work on the Cyborgs?" Nourse asked.

"Then they could escape once more," Schruille said. He shrugged. "What does it matter?"

"Into another megalopolis," Nourse said. "Is that it?"

"We know the infection's widespread," Schruille said.

"Certainly, there were cells right here in Central. We've cleaned out those, but the—"

"I say stop them now!" Nourse snapped.

"I agree with Schruille," Calapine said. "What's the risk?"

"The sooner we stop them the sooner we can return to our own pursuits," Nourse said.

"This *is* our pursuit," Schruille said.

"You like the idea of sterilizing another megalopolis, don't you, Schruille?" Nourse sneered. "Which one this time? How about Loovil?"

"Once was enough," Schruille said. "But likes and dislikes really have nothing to do with it."

"Let us put it to a vote then," Calapine said.

"Because you're two to one against me, eh?" Nourse said.

"She means a *full* vote," Schruille said. He looked up at the observation lights. "We've obviously a full quorum."

Nouse stared at the indicators knowing he'd been neatly trapped. He dared not protest a full vote—any vote. And his two companions appeared so sure of themselves. *"This is our pursuit."*

"We've allowed the Cyborgs to interfere," Nourse said, "because they increased the proportion of viables in the genetic reserve. Did we do this merely to destroy the genetic reserve?"

Schruille indicated a bank of binary pyramids on the Globe's wall. "If they endanger us, certainly. But the issue is unregistered *self*-viables, their possible immunity to the contraceptive gas. Where else could they have produced the substitute embryo?"

"If it comes down to it, we don't need any of them," Calapine said.

"Destroy them all?" Nourse asked. "All the Folk?"

"And raise a new crop of dopplegangers," she said. "Why not?"

"Duplicates don't always come true," Nourse said.

"Nothing limits us," Schruille said.

"Our sun isn't infinite," Nourse said.

"We'll solve that when the need arises," Calapine said. "What problem can defy us? We're not limited by time."

"Yet we're sterile," Nourse said. "Our gametes refuse to unite."

"And well they do," Schruille said. "I'd not have it otherwise."

"All we wish now is a simple vote," Calapine said. "A simple vote on whether to capture and bring in one tiny band of criminals. Why should that arouse major debate?"

Nourse started to speak, thought better of it. He shook his head, looked from Calapine to Schruille.

"Well?" Schruille asked.

"I think this little band is the real issue," Nourse said. "One Sterrie surgeon, two Cyborgs and two viables."

"And Durant was ready to kill the Sterrie," Schruille said.

"No." It was Calapine. "He wasn't ready to erase anyone." She found herself suddenly interested in the train of Nourse's reasoning. It was his logic and reason, after all, which had always attracted her.

Schruille, seeing her waver, said, "Calapine!"

"We all saw Durant's emotions," Nourse said. He waved at the instrument wall in front of him. "He would've killed no one. He was . . . *educating* Svengaard, talking to Svengaard with his hands."

"As they do between themselves, he and his wife," Calapine said. "Certainly!"

"You say we should raise a new crop of dopplegangers." Nourse said. "Which seed shall we use? The occupants of Seatac, perhaps?"

"We could take the seed cells first," Schruille said, and he wondered how he had been put so suddenly on the defensive. "I say let's vote on it. Bring them here for full interrogation or destroy them."

"No need," Nourse said. "I've changed my mind. Bring them here . . . if you can."

"Then it's settled," Schruille said. He rapped the signal into his throne arm. "You see, it's really very simple."

"Indeed?" Nourse said. "Then why do Calapine and I find ourselves suddenly reluctant to use violence? Why do we long for the old ways when Max shielded us from ourselves?"

19

The Hall of Counsel had not seen such a gathering since the debate over legalizing limited Cyborg experiments on their own kind some thirty thousand years before. The Optimen occupied a rainbow splashing of multicolored cushions on the banks of plasmeld benches. Some appeared nude, but most out of awareness of such a gathering's traditional nature came clothed in garments of their immediate historical whims. There were togas, kilts, gowns and ruffs, three-cornered hats and derbies, G-strings and muu-muus, fabrics and styles reaching back into pre-history.

Those who could not jam into the hall watched through half-a-million scanner eyes that glittered around the upper line of the walls.

It was barely daylight over Central, but not an Optiman slept.

The Survey Globe had been moved aside and the Tuyere occupied a position on the front bench center at the end of the hall. The prisoners had been brought in on a pneumoflot tumbril by acolytes. They sat on the tumbril's flat surface immobilized within dull blue plasmeld plastrons that permitted only the shallowest of breaths.

As she looked down on them from her bench, seeing the five figures so rigidly repressed, Calapine permitted herself a faint pity for them. The woman—such terror in her eyes. The rage in Harvey Durant's face. The resigned waiting in Glisson and Boumour. And Svengaard—a look of wary awakening.

Yet Calapine felt something was missing here. She couldn't name the missing thing, felt it only as a negative blankness within herself.

Nourse is right, she thought. *These five are important.*

Some Optiman up near the front of the hall had brought a tinkle-player and its little bell music could be heard above the murmurous whispering of the throng in the hall. The sound appeared to grow louder as the Optimen quieted in anticipation. The tinkle-player was stilled in mid-melody.

It grew quieter and quieter in the hall.

Despite her fear, Lizbeth stared around her in the growing silence. She had never before seen an Optiman in the flesh—only on the screens of the public announcement system. (In her lifetime it'd been mostly the members of the Tuyere, although older Folk mentioned the Kagiss trio preceding them.) They looked so varied and colorful—and so distant. She had the demoralizing feeling that nothing of this moment had happened by chance, that there was a terrifying symmetry in being here, now with this company.

"They are completely immobilized," Schruille said. "There's nothing to fear."

"Yet they are terrified," Nourse said. And he recalled suddenly a moment out of his youth. He'd been taken to an antiquary's home, one of the Hedonists proudly displaying his plasmeld copies of lost statues. There'd been a giant fish, one headless figure on a horse (very daring, that), a hooded monk and a man and woman clasped in a mutual embrace of terror. The man and woman, he realized now, had been recalled by the faces of Lizbeth and Harvey Durant.

They are, in a way, our parents, Nourse thought. *We spring from the Folk.*

Calapine realized abruptly what it was she missed here. There was no Max. He was gone, she knew, and she wondered momentarily what had happened to him. Outgrew his usefulness, she decided. The new Max must not be ready yet.

Odd that Max should go just like that, she thought. *But the lives of the Folk were like gossamer. One day you saw them; the next day you saw through the place where they had been. I must ask what happened to Max.* But she knew she wouldn't ever get around to that. The answer might require a disgusting word, a concept where even euphemisms would be repellent.

"Pay particular attention to the Cyborg Glisson," Schruille said. "Isn't it strange that our instruments reflect no emotions from him?"

"Perhaps he has no emotions," Calapine said.

"Hah!" Schruille barked. "Very good."

"I don't trust him," Nourse said. "My grandsire spoke of Cyborg tricks."

"He's virtually a robot," Schruille said. "Programed to respond with the closest precise answer to preserve his being. His present docility is interesting."

"Isn't it our purpose to interrogate them?" Nourse asked.

"In a moment," Schruille said. "We will peel them down to the raw brain and open their memories to our examination. First, it is well to study them."

"You're so callous, Schruille," Calapine said.

A murmurous agreement spread upward through the hall.

Schruille glanced at her. Calapine's voice had sounded so strange then. He found himself filled with a sudden disquiet.

Glisson's Cyborg eyes moved, heavy-lidded, coldly probing, glistening with their lensed alterations that expanded his spectrum of visibility.

"Do you see it, Durant?" he asked, his voice chopped into bits by the necessity of short breaths.

Harvey found his voice. "I . . . can't . . . believe . . . it."

"They are talking," Calapine said, her voice bright. She looked at the Durant male, surprised a look of loathing and pity in his eyes.

Pity? she wondered.

A glance at the tiny repeater bracelet on her wrist, confirmed the assessment of the Survey Globe. *Pity. Pity! How dare he pity me!*

"Har . . . vey," Lizbeth whispered.

Frustrated rage contorted Harvey's face. He moved his eyes, could not quite swing them far enough to see her. "Liz," he muttered. "Liz, I love you."

"This is a time for hate, not love," Glisson said, his detached tone giving the words an air of unreality. "Hate and revenge," Glisson said.

"What are you saying?" Svengaard asked. He'd listened with mounting amazement to their words. For a time, he'd thought of pleading with the Optimen that he'd been a prisoner, held against his will; but a sixth sense told him the attempt would be useless. He was nothing to these lordly creatures. He was foam in the backwash of a wave at a cliff base. They were the cliff.

"Look at them as a doctor," Glisson said. "They are dying."

"It's true," Harvey said.

Lizbeth had pressed her eyes closed against tears. Now, her eyes sprang open and she stared up at the people around her, seeing them through Harvey's eyes and Glisson's.

"They *are* dying," she breathed.

It was there for the trained eyes of an Underground courier to read. Mortality on the faces of the immortals! Glisson had seen it, of course, through his Cyborg abilities to see and respond, read-and-reflect.

"The Folk are *so* disgusting at times," Calapine said.

"They can't be," Svengaard said. There was an unreadable tone in his voice and Lizbeth wondered at it. The voice lacked the despair she could have expected.

"I say they *are* disgusting!" Calapine intoned. "No mere pharmacist should contradict me."

Boumore stirred out of a profound lethargy. The asyet alien computer logic within him had recorded the conversation, replayed it, derived corollary meanings. He looked up now as a new and partial Cyborg, read the subtle betrayals in Optiman flesh. The thing was there! Something had gone wrong with the live-forevers. The shock of it left

Boumour with a half-formed feeling of emptiness, as though he ought to respond with some emotion for which he no longer had the capacity.

"Their words," Nourse said. "I find their conversation mostly meaningless. What is it they're saying, Schruille?"

"Let us ask them now about the self-viables," Calapine said. "And the substitute embryo. Don't forget the substitute embryo."

"Look up there in the top row," Glisson said. "The tall one. See the wrinkles on his face?"

"He looks so old," Lizbeth whispered. She felt a curiously empty feeling. As long as the Optimen were there—unchangeable, eternal—her world contained a foundation that could never tremble. Even as she'd opposed them, she'd felt this. Cyborgs died . . . eventually. The Folk died. But Optimen went on and on and on . . .

"What is it?" Svengaard asked. "What's happening to them?"

"Second row on the left," Glisson said. "The woman with red hair. See the sunken eyes, the stare?"

Boumour moved his eyes to see the woman. Flaws in Optiman flesh leaped out as his gaze traversed the short arc permitted him.

"What're they saying?" Calapine demanded. "What is this?" Her voice sounded querulous even to her own ears. She felt fretful, annoyed by vague aches.

A muttering sound of discontent moved upward through the benches. There were little pockets of giggling and bursts of peevish anger, laughter.

We're supposed to interrogate these criminals, Calapine thought. *When will it start? Must I begin it?*

She looked at Schruille. He had scrunched down in his seat, glaring at Harvey Durant. She turned to Nourse, encountered a supercilious half-smile on his face, a remote look in his eyes. There was a throbbing at Nourse's neck she had never noticed before. A mottled patch of red veins stood out on his cheek.

They leave everything to me, she thought.

With a fretful movement of her shoulders, she touched

her bracelet controls. Lambent purple light washed over the giant globe at the side of the hall. A beam of the light spilled out from the globe's top as though decanted onto the floor. It reached out toward the prisoners.

Schruille watched the play of light. Soon the prisoners would be raw, shrieking creatures, he knew, spilling out all their knowledge for the Tuyere's instruments to analyze. Nothing would remain of them except nerve fibers along which the burning light would spread, drinking memories, experiences, knowledge.

"Wait!" Nourse said.

He studied the light. It had stopped its reaching movement toward the prisoners at his command. He felt they were making some gross error known only to himself and he looked around the abruptly silent hall wondering if any of the others could identify the error or speak it. Here was all the secret machinery of their government, everything planned, ordained. Somehow, the inelegant unexpectedness of naked Life had entered here. It was an error.

"Why do we wait?" Calapine asked.

Nourse tried to remember. He knew he had opposed this action. Why?

Pain!

"We must not cause pain," he said. "We must give them the chance to speak without duress."

"They've gone mad," Lizbeth whispered.

"And we've won," Glisson said. "Through my eyes, all my fellows can see—we've won."

"They're going to destroy us," Boumour said.

"But we've won," Glisson said.

"How?" Svengaard asked. And louder: "How?"

"We offered them Potter as bait and gave them a taste of violence," Glisson said. "We knew they'd look. They had to look."

"Why?" Svengaard whispered.

"Because we've changed the environment," Glisson said. "Little things, a pressure here, a shocking Cyborg there. And we gave them a taste for war."

"How?" Svengaard asked. "How?"

"Instinct," Glisson said. The word carried a computed finality, a sense of inhuman logic from which there was no escape. "War's an instinct with humans. Battle. Violence. But their systems have been maintained in delicate balance for so many thousands of years. Ah, the price they paid— tranquillity, detachment, boredom. Comes now violence with its demands and their ability to change has atrophied. They're heterodyning, swaying farther and farther from that line of perpetual life. Soon they'll die."

"War?" Svengaard had heard the stories of the violence from which the Optimen preserved the Folk. "It can't be," he said. "There's some new disease or—"

"I have stated the fact as computed to its ultimate decimal of logic," Glisson said.

Calapine screamed, "What're they saying?"

She could hear the prisoners' words distinctly, but their meaning eluded her. They were speaking obscenities. She heard a word, registered it, but the next word replaced it in her awareness without linkage. There was no intelligent sequence. Only obscenities. She rapped Schruille's arm. "What are they saying?"

"In a moment we will question them and discover," Schruille said.

"Yes," Calapine said. "The very thing."

"How is it possible?" Svengaard breathed. He could see two couples dancing on the benches high up at the back of the hall. There were couples embracing, making love. Two Optimen began shouting at each other on his right—nose to nose. Svengaard felt that he was watching buildings fall, the earth open and spew forth flames.

"Watch them!" Glisson said.

"Why can't they just compensate for this . . . change?" Svengaard demanded.

"Their ability to compensate is atrophied," Glisson said. "And you must understand that compensation itself is a new environment. It creates even greater demands. Look at them! They're oscillating out of control right now."

"Make them shut up!" Calapine shouted. She leaped to her feet, advanced on the prisoners.

Harvey watched, fascinated, terrified. There was a disjointed quality in her movement, in every response—except her anger. Rage burned at him from her eyes. A violent trembling swept through his body.

"You!" Calapine said, pointing at Harvey. "Why do you stare at me and mumble? Answer!"

Harvey found himself frozen in silence, not by his fear of her anger, but by a sudden overwhelming awareness of Calapine's age. How old was she? Thirty thousand years? Forty thousand? Was she one of the originals—eighty thousand or more years old?

"Speak up and say what you will," Calapine commanded. "I, Calapine, order it. Show honor now and perhaps we will be lenient."

Harvey stared, mute. She seemed unaware of the growing uproar all around.

"Durant," Glisson said, "you must remember there are subterranean things called instincts which direct destiny with the inexorable flow of a river. This is change. See it around us. Change is the only constant."

"But she's dying," Harvey said.

Calapine couldn't make sense of his words, but she found herself touched by the tone of concern for her in his voice. She consulted her bracelet linkage with the globe. *Concern!* He was worried about her, about Calapine, not about himself or his futile mate!

She turned into an oddly enfolding darkness, collapsed full length on the floor with her arms outstretched toward the benches.

A mirthless chuckle escaped Glisson's lips.

"We have to do something for them," Harvey said. "They have to understand what they're doing to themselves!"

Schruille stirred suddenly, looked up at the opposite wall, saw dark patches where scanners had been deactivated, abandoned by the Optimen who couldn't jam into the hall. He felt an abrupt alarm at the eddies of movement in the crowd all around. Some of the people were leaving—swaying, drifting, running, laughing, giggling. . . .

But we came to question the prisoners, Schruille thought.

The hysteria in the hall slowly impressed itself on Schruille's senses. He looked at Nourse.

Nourse sat with eyes closed, mumbling to himself. "Boiling oil," Nourse said. "But that's too sudden. We need something more subtle, more enduring."

Schruille leaned forward. "I have a question for the man Harvey Durant."

"What is it?" Nourse asked. He opened his eyes, pushed forward, subsided.

"What did he hope to gain by his actions?" Schruille asked.

"Very good," Nourse said. "Answer the question, Harvey Durant."

Nourse touched his own bracelet. The purple beam of light inched closer to the prisoners.

"I didn't want you to die," Harvey said. "Not this."

"Answer the question!" Schruille blared.

Harvey swallowed. "I wanted to—"

"We wanted to have a family," Lizbeth said. She spoke clearly, reasonably. "That's all. We wanted to be a family." Tears started in her eyes and she wondered then what her child would have been like. Certainly, none of them were going to survive this madness.

"What is this?" Schruille asked. "What is this family nonsense?"

"Where did you get the substitute embryo?" Nourse asked. "Answer and we may be lenient." Again the burning light moved toward the prisoners.

"We have self-viables immune to the contraceptive gas," Glisson said. "Many of them."

"You see?" Schruille said. "I told you so."

"Where are these self-viables?" Nourse asked. He felt his right hand trembling, looked at it wonderingly.

"Right under your noses," Glisson said. "Scattered through the population. And don't ask me to identify them. I don't know them all. No one does."

"None will escape us," Schruille said.

"None!" Nourse echoed.

"If we must," Schruille said, "we'll sterilize all but Central and start over."

"With what will you start over?" Glisson asked.

"What?" Schruille screamed the word at the Cyborg.

"Where will you find the genetic pool from which to start over?" Glisson asked. "You are sterile—and terminating."

"We need but one cell to duplicate the original," Schruille said, his voice sneering.

"They why haven't you duplicated yourselves?" Glisson asked.

"You dare question us?" Nourse demanded.

"I will answer for you then," Glisson said. "You've not chosen duplication because the doppleganger is unstable. The trend of the duplicates is downward—extinction."

Calapine heard scattered words—"Sterile . . . terminating . . . unstable . . . extinction . . ." They were hideous words that crept down into the depths where she lay watching a string of fat sausages parade in glowing order before her awareness. They were like seeds with a lambent radiance moving against a background of oiled black velvet. Sausages. Seeds. She saw them then not precisely as seeds, but as encapsulated life—walled in, shielded, bridging a period unfavorable to life. It made the idea of seeds less repellent to her. They were life . . . always life.

"We don't need the genetic pool," Schruille said.

Calapine heard his voice clearly, felt she could read his thoughts. Words out of one of the glowing sausages forced themselves upon her: *We have our millions in Central. We are enough by ourselves. Feeble, short-lived Folk are a disgusting reminder of our past. They are pets and we no longer need pets.*

"I've decided what we can do to these criminals," Nourse said. He spoke loudly to force his voice over the growing hubbub in the hall. "We will apply nerve excitation a micron at a time. The pain will be exquisite and can be drawn out for centuries."

"But you said you didn't want to cause pain," Schruille shouted.

"Didn't I?" Nourse's voice sounded worried.

I don't feel well, Calapine thought. *I need a long session in the pharmacy. Pharmacy.* The word was a switch that turned on her consciousness. She felt her body stretched out on the floor, pain and wetness at her nose where it had struck the floor in her fall.

"Your suggestion contains some merit, however," Schuiller said. "We could restore the nerves behind our ministrations and carry on the punishment indefinitely. Exquisite pain forever!"

"A hell," Nourse said. "Appropriate."

"They're insane enough to do it," Svengaard rasped. "How can we stop them?"

"Glisson!" Lizbeth said. "Do something!"

But the Cyborg remained silent.

"This is something you didn't anticipate, isn't it, Glisson?" Svengaard said.

Still, the Cyborg held to silence.

"Answer me!" Svengaard grated.

"They were just supposed to die," Glisson said, voice dispassionate.

"But now they could sterilize all the earth except Central and go on in their madness by themselves," Svengaard said. "And *we* could be tortured forever!"

"Not forever," Glisson said. "They're dying."

A cheer went up from the Optimen at the rear of the hall. None of the prisoners could turn to see what had aroused the sound, but it added a new dimension to the sense of urgency around them.

Calapine lifted herself from the floor. Her nose and mouth throbbed with pain. She turned toward the tumbril, saw a commotion among the Optimen beyond it. They were leaping on benches to watch some excited activity hidden in their midst. A naked body lifted suddenly above the throng, turned over and went down again with a sodden thump. Again, a cheer shook the hall.

What're they doing? Calapine wondered. *They're hurting each other—themselves.*

She wiped a hand across her nose and mouth, looked at the hand. Blood. She could smell it now, a tantalizing

smell. Her own blood. It fascinated her. She crossed to the
prisoners, showed the hand to Harvey Durant.

"Blood," she said. She touched her nose. Pain! "It hurts,"
she said. "Why does it hurt, Harvey Durant?" She stared
into his eyes. Such sympathy in his eyes. He was human.
He cared.

Harvey looked at her, their eyes almost level because of
the tumbril's position above the floor. He felt a profound
compassion for her suddenly. She was Lizbeth; she was
Calapine; she was all women. He saw the concentrated intensity of her attention, the here-now awareness which
excluded everything except her need for his words.

"It hurts me, too, Calapine," he said, "but your death
would hurt me more."

For an instant, Calapine thought the hall had grown still
around her. She realized then that noises of the throng continued unabated. She could hear Nourse chanting, "Good!
Good!" and Schruille saying, "Excellent! Excellent!" She
realized then that she had been the only one to hear Durant's hideous words. It was blasphemy. She'd lived
thousands of years suppressing the very concept of personal
death. It could not be said or conceived in the mind. But
she had *heard* the words. She wanted to turn away, to believe those words had never happened. But something of
the attention she had focused on Harvey Durant held her
chained to his meaning. Only minutes ago, she had been
where the seed of life spanned the eons. She had felt the
wild presence of forces that could move within the mito-
chrondrial structures of the cells.

"Please," Lizbeth whispered. "Free us. You're a woman.
You must have some compassion. What have we done to
harm you? Is it wrong to want love and life? We didn't
want to harm you."

Calapine gave no sign that she heard. There were only
Harvey's words playing over and over in her mind, *"Your
death . . . your death . . . your death . . . your death . . ."*

Odd flickerings of heat and chill surged through her
body. She heard another cheer from the crowd in the far
benches. She felt her own sickness and growing awareness

of the cul-de-sac in which she had been trapped. Anger suffused her. She bent to the tumbril's controls, punched a button beneath Glisson.

The carapaces of the shell which held the Cyborg began closing. Glisson's eyes opened wide. A rasping moan escaped him. Calapine giggled, punched another button on the controls. The shells snapped to their former position. Glisson gasped.

She turned to the controls beneath Harvey, poised a finger over the buttons. "Explain your disgusting breach of manners!"

Harvey remained frozen in silence. She was going to crush him!

Svengaard began to laugh. He knew his own position, the first-class second-rater. Why had he been chosen for this moment—to see Glisson and Boumour without words, Nourse and Schruille babbling on their bench, the Optimen in little knots and eddies of mad violence, Calapine ready to kill her prisoners and doubtless forget it ten seconds later. His laughter went out of control.

"Stop that laughing!" Calapine screamed.

Svengaard trembled with hysteria. He gasped for breath. The shock of her voice helped him gain a measure of control, but it still was immensely ludicrous.

"Fool!" Calapine said. "Explain yourself."

Svengaard stared at her. He could feel only pity now. He remembered the sea from the medical resort at Lapush and he thought he saw now why the Optimen had chosen this place so far from any ocean. Instinct. The sea produced waves, surf—a constant reminder that they had set themselves against eternity's waves. They could not face that.

"Answer me," Calapine said. Her hand hovered above his shell's controls.

Svengaard could only stare at her and at the Optimen in their madness beyond her. They stood exposed before him as though their bodies had been opened to spill twisting entrails on the floor.

They have souls with only one scar, Svengaard thought. It was carved on them day by day, century by century,

eon by eon—the increment of panic that their blessed for-
everness might be illusion, that it might after all have an
ending. He had never before suspected the price the Optimen paid for infinity. The more of it they possessed, the
greater its value. The greater the value, the greater the fear
of losing it. The pressure went up and up . . . forever.

But there had to be a breaking point. The Cyborgs had
seen this, and in their emotionless manner had missed the
real consequences.

The Optimen had themselves hemmed in with euphemisms. They had pharmacists, not doctors, because doctors
meant sickness and injury, and that equaled the unthinkable. They had only their pharmacy and its countless outlets
never more than a few steps from any Optiman. They never
left Central and its elaborate safeguards. They existed as
perpetual adolescents in their nursery prison.

"So you won't speak," Calapine said.

"Wait," Svengaard said as her hand moved toward the
buttons beneath him. "When you've killed all the viables
and only you remain, when you see yourselves dying one
by one, what then?"

"How dare you?" she said. "You think to question an
Optiman whose experience of life makes yours no more
than that!" She snapped her fingers.

He looked at her bruised nose, the blood.

"Optiman," Svengaard said. "A Sterrie whose constitu-
tion will accept the enzyme adjustment for infinite life . . .
until destruction comes from within. I think you want to
die."

Calapine drew herself up, glared at him. As she did, she
became aware of a sudden odd silence in the hall. She
swept a glance around her, saw intent watchfulness in every
eye focused upon her. Realization came slowly. *They see
the blood on my face.*

"You had infinite life," Svengaard said. "Does that make
you necessarily more brilliant, more intelligent? No. You
merely lived longer, had more time for experience and education. Very likely, most of you are educated beyond your
intelligence, else you'd have seen long ago that this mo-

ment was inevitable—the delicate balance destroyed, all of you dying."

Calapine took a step backward. His words were like painful knives burning into her nerves.

"Look at you!" Svengaard said. "All of you sick. What does your precious pharmacy do? I know without being told: It prescribes wider and wider variant prescriptions, more frequent dosages. It's trying to check the oscillations because that's how it's programmed. It'll go on trying as long as you permit it, but it won't save you."

Someone screamed behind her, "Silence him!"

The cry was taken up around the hall, a deafening chant, foot stamping, hands pounding, "Si-lence him! Si-lence him! Si-lence him!"

Calapine pressed her hands to her ears. She could still feel the chant through her skin. And now she saw Optimen start down off the benches toward the prisoners. She knew bloody violence was only a heartbeat away.

They stopped.

She couldn't understand why, and dropped her hands away from her ears. Screams rained down on her. The names of half-forgotten dieties were invoked. Eyes stared at something on the floor at the head of the hall.

Calapine whirled, saw Nourse writhing there, foamy spittle around his mouth. His skin was a mottled reddish purple and yellow. Clawed hands reached out, scraped the floor.

"Do something!" Svengaard shouted. "He's dying!" Even as he shouted, he felt the strangeness of his words. *Do something!?* His medical training surfaced and spoke no matter what happened.

Calapine backed away, put out her hands in a warding gesture as old as witchcraft. Schruille leaped up, stood on the bench where he'd been sitting. His mouth moved soundlessly.

"Calapine," Svengaard said, "if you won't help him, release me so I can do it."

She leaped to obey, filled with gratitude that she could give this hideous responsibility to another.

The restraining shells fell away at her touch. Svengaard

leaped down, almost fell. His legs and arms tingled from
the long confinement. He limped toward Nourse, his eyes
and mind working as he moved. *Mottled yellow in the
skin—most probably an immune reaction to pantothenic
acid and a failure of adrenalin suppression.*

The red triangle of a pharmacy outlet glowed on the wall
at his left above the benches. Svengaard stooped, picked
up Nourse's writhing form, began climbing toward the
symbol. The man was a sudden death weight in his arms,
no movement except a shallow lifting of the breast.

Optimen fell back from him as though he carried plague.
Abruptly, someone above him shouted, "Let me out!"

The mob turned away. Feet pounded on the plasmeld.
They jammed up at the exits, clawed and climbed over one
another. There were screams, curses, hoarse shouts. It was
like a cattle pen with a predator loose in the midst of the
animals.

Part of Svengaard's awareness registered on a woman at
his right. He passed her. She lay stretched across two banks
of seats, her back at an odd angle, mouth gaping, eyes staring, blood on her arms and neck. There was no sign of
breath. He climbed past a man who dragged himself up the
tiered benches, one leg useless, his eyes intent on an exit
sign and a doorway which appeared to be filled with writhing shapes.

Svengaard's arms ached from his load. He stumbled, almost fell up the last two steps as he eased Nourse to the
floor beside the pharmacy outlet.

There were voices down behind him now—Durant and
Boumour shouting to be released.

Later, Svengaard thought. He put his hand to the door
control on the pharmacy outlet. The doors refused to open.
Of course, he thought. *I'm not an Optiman.* He lifted
Nourse, put one of the Optiman's hands to the control. The
doors slid aside. Behind them lay what appeared to be the
standard presentation of a priority rack—pyrimidines, aneurin . . .

Aneurin and inositol, he thought. *Got to counteract the
immune reaction.*

A familiar flow-analysis board occupied the right side with a gap for insertion of an arm and the usual vampire needles protruding from their gauges. Svengaard tripped the keys on the master flow gauge, opened the panel. He traced back the aneurin and inositol feeders, immobilized the others, thrust Nourse's arm beneath the needles. They found veins, dipped into flesh. Gauges kicked over.

Svengaard pinched off the return line to stop feedback. Again, the gauges kicked over.

Gently, Svengaard disengaged Nourse's arm from the needles, stretched him on the floor. His face was now a uniform pale white, but his breathing had deepened. His eyelids flickered. His flesh felt cold, clammy.

Shock, Svengaard thought. He removed his own jacket, put it around Svengaard, began massaging the arms to restore circulation.

Calapine came into view on his right, sat down at Nourse's head. Her hands were clasped tightly together, knuckles white. There was an odd clarity in her face, the eyes with a look of staring into distances. She felt she had come a much farther distance than up from the floor of the hall, drawn by memories that would not be denied. She knew she had gone through madness into an oddly detached sanity.

The red ball of the Survey Globe caught her eye, the egg of enormous power that did her bidding even now. She thought about Nourse, her many-times playmate. Playmate and toys.

"Will he die?" she asked. She turned to watch Svengaard.

"Not immediately," Svengaard said. "But that final burst of hysteria . . . he's done irreparable damage to his system."

He grew aware that there were only muted moans and a very few controlled commands in the hall now. Some of the acolytes had rallied to help.

"I released Boumour and the Durants and sent a plea for more . . . medical help," Calapine said. "There are a number of . . . dead . . . many injured."

Dead, she thought. *What an odd word to apply to an Optiman. Dead . . . dead . . . dead . . .*

She felt then how necessity had forced her into a new kind of living awareness, a new rhythm. It had happened down there in a burst of memories that trailed through forty thousand years. None of it escaped her—not a moment of kindness nor of brutality. She remembered all the Max Allgoods, Seatac . . . every lover, every toy . . . Nourse.

Svengaard glanced around at a shuffling sound, saw Boumour approaching with a woman limp in his arms. There was a blue bruise across her cheek and jaw. Her arms hung like sticks.

"Is this pharmacy outlet available?" Boumour asked. His voice held that chilled Cyborg quality, but there was shock in his eyes and a touch of horror.

"You'll have to operate the board manually," Svengaard said. "I keyed out the demand system, jammed the feedback."

Boumour stepped heavily around him with the woman. How fragile she looked. A vein pulsed thickly at her neck.

"I must concoct a muscle relaxant until we can get her to a hospital," Boumour said. "She broke her own arms—contramuscular strain."

Calapine recognized the face, remembered they had disputed mildly about a man once—about a playmate.

Svengaard moved to Nourse's right arm, continued massaging. The move brought the floor of the hall into view and the tumbril. Glisson sat impassively armless in his restraining shell. Lizbeth lay at one side with Harvey kneeling beside her.

"Mrs. Durant!" Svengaard said, remembering his obligation.

"She's all right," Boumour said. "Immobilization for the past few hours was the best thing that could've happened to her."

Best thing! Svengaard thought. *Durant was right: These Cyborgs are as insensitive as machines.*

"Si-lence him," Nourse whispered.

Svengaard looked down at the pale face, saw the broken veins in the cheeks, the sagging, unresponsive flesh. Nourse's eyelids flickered open.

"Leave him to me," Calapine said.

Nourse moved his head, tried to look at her. He blinked, having obvious trouble focusing. His eyes began to water.

Calapine lifted his head, slid under him until he rested on her lap. She began stroking his brow.

"He used to like this," she said. "Go help the others, Doctor."

"Cal," Nourse said. "Oh, Cal . . . I . . . hurt."

20

Why do you help them?" Glisson asked. "I don't understand you, Boumour. Your actions aren't logical. What use is it to help them?"

He looked up through the open segment of the Survey
Globe at Calapine sitting alone on the dais of the Tuyere.
The lights of the interior played a slow rhythm across her
face. A glowing pyramid of projected binaries danced on
the air in front of her.

Glisson had been released from his shell of restraint, but
he still sat on the tumbril, his arm connections dangling
empty. A medicouch had been brought in for Lizbeth Durant. She lay on it with Harvey seated beside her. Boumour
stood with his back to Glisson, looking up into the globe.
His fingers moved nervously, clenching, opening. There
was a streak of dried blood down his right sleeve. The elfin
face held a look of puzzlement.

Svengaard came in from behind the globe, a slowly moving figure in the red shadows. Abruptly, the hall glared with
light. The main globes had gone on automatically as darkness fell outside. Svengaard stopped to check Lizbeth, patted Harvey's shoulder. "She will be all right. She's strong."

Lizbeth's eyes followed him as he moved around to look
into the Survey Globe. Svengaard's shoulders sagged with

fatigue, but there was a look of elation in his face. He was
a man who'd found himself.

"Calapine," Svengaard said, "that was the last of them
going out to hospitals."

"I see it," she said. She looked up at the scanners, every
one lighted. Somewhat more than half of the Optimen were
under restraint—mad. Thousands had died. More thousands
lay sorely injured. Those who remained watched their
globe. She sighed, wondering at their thoughts, wondering
how they faced the fact that all had fallen from the tight
wire of immortality. Her own emotions confused her. There
was an odd feeling of relief in her breast.

"What of Schruille?" she asked.

"Crushed at a door," Svengaard said. "He's . . . dead."
She sighed. "And Nourse?"

"Responding to treatment."

"Don't you understand what's happened to you?" Glisson demanded. His eyes glittered as he stared up at Calapine.

Calapine looked down at him, spoke clearly, "We've un-
dergone an emotional stress that has altered the delicate
balance of our metabolism," she said. "You tricked us into
it. The evidence is quite clear—there's no turning back."

"Then you understand," Glisson said. "Any attempt to
force your systems back into the old forms will result in
boredom and a gradual descent into apathy."

Calapine smiled. "Yes, Glisson. We'd not want that.
We've been addicted to a new kind of . . . aliveness that we
didn't know existed."

"Then you do understand," Glisson said and there was a
grudging quality to his voice.

"We broke the rhythm of life," Calapine said. "All life
is immersed in rhythm, but we got out of step. I suppose
that was the *outside* interference in those embryos—rhythm
asserting itself."

"Well then," Glisson said, "the sooner you can turn
things over to us, the sooner things will settle down into—"

"To you?" Calapine asked scornfully. She looked out
into the quick contrasts of the hall's glaring light. How

black and white it all was. "I'd sooner condemn us all,"
she said.

"But you're dying!"

"So are you," Calapine said.

Svengaard swallowed. He could see that the old animosities would not be suppressed easily. And he wondered at himself, a second-rater surgeon who had suddenly found himself as a doctor, ministering to people who needed him. Durant had seen *that*—the need to be needed.

"I may have a plan we could accept, Calapine," Svengaard said.

"To you we will listen," Calapine said, and there was affection in her voice. She studied Svengaard as he searched for words, remembering that this man had saved the lives of Nourse and many others.

We made no plans for the unthinkable, she thought, *Is it possible that this nobody who was once a target for kindly sneers can save us?* She dared not let herself hope.

"The Cyborgs have techniques for bringing the emotions into a more or less manageable stasis," Svengaard said. "Once that's done, I believe I know a way to dampen the enzymic oscillations in most of you."

Calapine swallowed. The scanner-eye lights above her began to flash as the watchers signaled for her to let them into the communications channels. They had questions, of course. She had questions of her own, but she didn't know that she could speak them. She caught a reflection of her own face in one of the prisms, was reminded of the look in Lizbeth's eyes as the woman had pleaded from the tumbril.

"I can't promise infinite life," Svengaard said, "but I believe many of you can have many more thousands of years."

"Why should we agree to help them?" Glisson demanded. There was a measuring quality in his voice, a hint of the querulous.

"You're failures, too!" Svengaard said. "Can't you see that?" He realized he had shouted with the full power of his disillusionment.

"Don't shout at me!" Glisson snapped.

So they do have emotions, Svengaard thought. *Pride . . . anger . . .*

"Are you still suffering under the delusion that you're in control of this situation?" Svengaard asked. He pointed to Calapine. "That one woman up there could still exterminate every non-Optiman on earth."

"Listen to him, you Cyborg fool," Calapine said.

"Let's not be too free with that word 'fool'," Svengaard said. He stared up at Calapine.

"Watch your tongue, Svengaard," Calapine said. "Our patience is not infinite."

"Nor is your gratitude, eh?" Svengaard said.

A bitter smile touched her mouth. "We were talking about survival," she said.

Svengaard sighed. He wondered then if the patterns of thought conditioned by the illusion of infinite life could ever be truly broken. She had spoken there like the old Tuyere. But her resiliency had surprised him before.

The outburst had touched Harvey's fears for Lizbeth. He glared at Svengaard and Glisson, tried to control his terror and rage. This hall awed him with its immensity and its remembered bedlam. The globe towered over him, a monstrous force that could crush them.

"Survival, then," Svengaard said.

"Let us understand each other," Calapine said. "There are those among us who will say that your help was merely our due. You are still our captives. There are those who'll demand you submit and reveal your entire Underground to us."

"Yes, let us understand each other," Svengaard said. "Who are your prisoners? Myself, a person who was not a member of the Underground and knows little about it. You have Glisson, who knows more, but assuredly not all. You have Boumour, one of your escaped *pharmacists,* who knows even less than Glisson. You have the Durants, whose knowledge probably goes little beyond their own cell group. What will you gain even if you milk us dry?"

"Your plan to save us," Calapine said.

"My plan requires cooperation, not coercion," Svengaard said.

"And it will only give us a continuation, not restore us to our original condition, is that it?" Calapine asked.

"You should welcome that," Svengaard said. "It would give you a chance to mature, become useful." He waved a hand to indicate their surroundings "You've frozen yourselves in immaturity here! You've played with toys! I'm offering you a chance to live!"

Is that it? Calapine wondered. *Is this new aliveness a by-product of the knowledge that we must die?*

"I'm not at all sure we'll cooperate," Glisson said.

Harvey had had enough. He leaped to his feet, glared at Glisson. "You want the human race to die, you robot! You! You're another dead end!"

"Prattle!" Glisson said.

"Listen," Calapine said. She began sampling the communications channels. Bits of sentences poured out into the hall:

"We can restore enzymic balance with our own resources!" . . . "Eliminate these creatures!" . . . "What's his plan? What's his plan?" . . . "Begin the sterilization!" . . . ". . . his plan?" . . . "How long do we have if . . ." . . . "There's no doubt we can . . ."

Calapine silenced the voices with a flick of a switch. "It will be put to a vote," she said. "I remind you of that."

"You will die, and soon, if we don't cooperate," Glisson said. "I want that fully understood."

"You know Svengaard's plan?" Calapine asked.

"His thought patterns are transparent," Glisson said.

"I think not," Calapine said. "I saw him work on Nourse. He manipulated a dispensary to produce a dangerous overdose of aneurin and inostol. Remembering that, I ask myself how many of us will die in the attempt to arrest this process we can all feel within ourselves? Would I have risked such an overdose upon myself? How does this relate to the excitement we feel? Will any of us, having tasted excitement, wish to sink back into a non-emotional . . .

boredom?" She looked at Svengaard. "These are some of my questions."

"I know his plan," Glisson sneered. "Quell your emotions and implant an enzymic dispensary within each of you. Make Cyborgs of you." A tight grin etched a line of teeth in Glisson's face. "It's your only hope. Accepting it, you will have lost to us at last."

Calapine glared down at him, shocked.

Harvey was caught by the carping meanness in Glisson's voice. His own schism from the Underground had always known the Cyborgs were too calculating and narrow-minded to be trusted with purely human decisions, but he had never before seen the fact so clearly demonstrated.

"Is that your plan, Svengaard?" Calapine demanded.

Harvey jumped up. "No! That's not his plan!"

Svengaard nodded to himself. *Of course! A fellow human, and a father would know.*

"You pretend to know what I, a Cyborg, do not know?" Glisson asked.

Svengaard looked at Harvey with raised eyebrows.

"Embryos," Harvey said.

Svengaard nodded, looked up at Calapine. "I propose to keep you continually implanted with living embryos," he said. "Living monitors that will make you adjust to your own needs. You will regain your emotions, your . . . zest for life, this excitement you prize."

"You propose to make of us living *vats for embryos?*" Calapine asked, wonder in her voice.

"The gestation process can be delayed for hundreds of years," Svengaard said. "With proper hormone adjustment, this can be applied even to men. Caesarian delivery, of course, but it need not be painful . . . or frequent."

Calapine weighed his words, wondering why she felt no disgust at the suggestion. Once she had felt disgust at the realization that Lizbeth Durant carried an embryo within her, but Calapine realized now her disgust had been compounded of jealousy. Not all the Optimen would accept this, she knew. Some would hope for a return to the old ways. She looked up at the globe's telltales. No one had escaped the poisoning excitement, though. They would have to understand that everyone was going to die . . . sooner or later. Choice of time was all they had.

We didn't have immortality after all, she thought, *only the illusion. We had that, though . . . for eons.*

"Calapine!" Glisson said. "You're not going to accept this—this foolish proposal?"

The mechanical man is outraged at a living solution, she thought. She said, "Boumour, what do you say?"

"Yes," Glisson said, "speak up, Boumour. Point out the illogicality of this . . . *proposal.*"

Boumour turned, studied Glisson, glanced at Svengaard, at the Durants, stared up at Calapine. There was a look of secret wisdom in Boumour's pinched face. "I can still remember . . . how it was," he said. "I . . . think it was better . . . before I . . . was changed."

"Boumour!" Glisson said.

Hit him in his pride, Svengaard thought.

Glisson glared up at Calapine with mechanical intensity. "It's not yet determined that we'll help you!"

"Who needs you?" Svengaard asked. "You've no monopoly on your techniques. You'd save a little time and trouble, that's all. We can find embryos."

Glisson stared from one to the other. "But this isn't the way it was computed! You're not supposed to help them!"

The Cyborg fell silent, eyes glassy.

"*Doctor* Svengaard," Calapine said, "could you give us elite, viable embryos such as the Durants'? You saw the arginine intrusion. Nourse believes this possible."

"It's possible," Svengaard said. He considered. "Yes, it's . . . probable."

Calapine looked up at the scanners. "If we accept this offer," she said, "we go on living. You feel it? We're alive now, but we can remember a recent time when we weren't alive."

"We'll help if we must," Glisson said, and there was that carping tone in his voice.

Only Lizbeth, realizing her own bucolic docility in pregnancy, recognizing the flattening tenor of her emotions, suspected the *logical* fact which had swayed the Cyborg. Docile people could be controlled. That's what Glisson was thinking. She could read it in him, understanding him fully for the first time now that she knew he had pride and anger.

Calapine, reading on the Survey Globe's wall the mounting pressure of a single question from her Optiman audience, set up the analogues for an answer. It came swiftly for the scanners to see, "This process could provide eight to twelve thousand years of additional life even for the Folk."

"Even for the Folk," Calapine whispered. They'd discover this, she knew. There could be no more Security now. Even the Survey Globe had been shown to have flaws and limits. Glisson knew it. She could tell this, reading his silent withdrawal down there. Svengaard certainly would realize it. Possibly even the Durants.

She looked at Svengaard, knowing what she had to do. It would be easy to lose the Folk in this moment, lose them completely.

"If it is done," Calapine said, "it will be done for anyone who wishes it—Folk or Optiman."

This is politics, she thought. *This is the way the Tuyere would do it . . . even Schruille. Especially Schruille. Clever Schruille. Dead Schruille.* She could almost hear him chuckling.

"Can it be done for the Folk?" Harvey asked.

"For anyone," she said, and she smiled at Glisson, letting him see how she'd won. "I think we can put it to a vote now."

Once more, she looked up at the scanners, wondering if she'd gauged her people correctly. Most of them would see what she'd done, of course. But there'd be some clinging to the hope they could restore complete enzymic balance. She knew better. Her body knew. But some might choose to try that dangerous course back to boredom and apathy.

"Green for acceptance of *Doctor* Svengaard's proposal," she said. "Gold against."

Slowly, then with cumulating speed, the circle of scanner lights changed color—green . . . green . . . great washes of

it with only here and there a dot or pocket of gold. It was
a more overwhelming acceptance than she'd expected and
this made her edgy, suspicious. She trusted her voting instincts. Overwhelming acceptance. She consulted the
Globe's instruments, read the presentation of the answer:
"The Cyborg can be maneuvered through its belief in the
omnipotence of logic."

Calapine nodded to herself, thinking of her madness. *And
Life cannot be totally maneuvered against the interests of
living*, she thought.

"The proposal is accepted," she said.

And she found she did not like the sudden *pouncing* look
on Glisson's face. *We've overlooked something*, she
thought. *But we'll find it . . . once we're newly adjusted.*

Svengaard turned to look at Harvey Durant, allowed himself a broad grin. This was like the operating room, he
thought. One shaped minutiae and the broad pattern followed. It could be done with precision even as it was done
down in the cell.

Harvey weighed Svengaard's grin, read the emotional
betrayals on the man's face. All the faces around him carried their own exposure in this instant, all open to be read
by a courier trained in the Underground. It was a stand-off
between the powerful. The Folk might yet have a chance—
thousands of years of chance, if Calapine were to be believed—and she believed it herself. The genetic environment had been shaped into a new pattern and he could see
it. This was an indefinite pattern, full of indeterminacy. Heisenberg would've liked this pattern. The movers themselves
had been moved—and changed—by moving.

"When can Lizbeth and I leave here?" Harvey asked.

*In the desert, the line between life and death
is sharp and quick.*

—Zensunni fire poetry from Arrakis

Far from thinking machines and the League of Nobles, the desert never changed. The Zensunni descendants who had fled to Arrakis scraped out squalid lives in isolated cave communities, barely subsisting in a harsh environment. They experienced little enjoyment, yet fought fiercely to remain alive for just another day.

Sunlight poured across the ocean of sand, warming dunes that rippled like waves breaking upon an imagined shore. A few black rocks poked out of the dust like islands, but offered no shelter from the heat or the demon worms.

This desolate landscape was the last thing he would ever see. The people had accused him, chosen the young man as a scapegoat, and would mete out their punishment. His innocence was not relevant.

"Begone, Selim!" came a shout from the caves above. "Go far from here!" He recognized the voice of his young friend—*former* friend—Ebrahim. Perhaps the other boy was relieved, since by rights it should have been him facing exile and death, not Selim. But no one would mourn the loss of an orphan, and so Selim had been cast out in the Zensunni version of justice.

A raspy voice said, "May the worms spit out your scrawny hide." That was old Glyffa, who had once been like a mother to him. "Thief! Water stealer!"

From the caves, the tribe began to throw stones. One sharp rock struck the cloth he had wrapped around his dark hair for protection against the sun. Selim ducked, but did not give them the satisfaction of seeing him cringe. They had stripped almost everything from him, but as long as he drew breath they would never take his pride.

Naib Dhartha, the sietch leader, leaned out. "The tribe has spoken. Your fate rests on your own crimes, Selim."

Protestations of his innocence would do no good, nor would excuses or explanations. Keeping his balance on the steep path, the young man stooped to grab a sharp-edged stone. He held it in his palm and glared up at the people.

Selim had always been skilled at throwing rocks. He could pick off ravens, small kangaroo mice, or lizards for the community cookpot. If he aimed carefully, he could have put out one of the Naib's eyes. Selim had seen Dhartha whispering quietly with Ebrahim's father, watched them form their plan to cast the blame on him instead of the guilty boy. They had decided Selim's punishment using measures other than the truth.

Naib Dhartha had dark eyebrows and jet-black hair bound into a ponytail by a dull metal ring. A purplish geometric tattoo of dark angles and straight lines marked his left cheek. His wife had drawn it on his face using a steel needle and the juice of a scraggly inkvine the Zensunni cultivated in their terrarium gardens. The Naib glared down as if daring Selim to throw the stone, because the Zensunni would respond with a pummeling barrage of large rocks.

But such a punishment would kill him far too quickly. Instead, the tribe would drive Selim away from their tight-knit community. And on Arrakis, one did not survive without help. Existence in the desert required cooperation, each person doing his part. The Zensunni looked upon stealing—especially the theft of water—as the worst crime imaginable.

Selim pocketed the stone. Ignoring the jeers and insults, he continued his tedious descent toward the open desert.

Dhartha intoned in a voice that sounded like a bass howl

of stormwinds, "Selim, who has no father or mother—Selim, who was welcomed as a member of our tribe—you have been found guilty of stealing tribal water. Therefore, you must walk across the sands." Dhartha raised his voice, shouting before the condemned man could pass out of earshot. "May Shaitan choke on your bones."

All his life, Selim had done more work than most others. Because he was of unknown parentage, the tribe demanded it of him. No one helped him when he was sick, except maybe old Glyffa; no one carried an extra load for him. He had watched some of his companions gorge themselves on inflated family shares of water, even Ebrahim. And still, the other boy, seeing half a literjon of brackish water untended, had drunk it, foolishly hoping no one would notice. How easy it had been for Ebrahim to blame it on his supposed friend when the theft was discovered. . . .

Upon driving Selim from the caves, Dhartha had refused to give him even a tiny water pouch for his journey, because that was considered a waste of tribal resources. None of them expected Selim to survive more than a day anyway, even if he somehow managed to avoid the fearsome monsters of the desert.

He muttered under his breath, knowing they couldn't hear him, "May your mouth fill with dust, Naib Dhartha." Selim bounded down the path away from the cliffs, while his people continued to utter curses from above. A hurled pebble bounced past him.

When he reached the base of the rock wall that stood as a shield against the desert and the sandworm demons, he set off in a straight line, wanting to get as far away as he could. Dry heat pounded on his head. Those watching him would surely be surprised to see him voluntarily hike out onto the dunes instead of huddling in a cave in the rocks.

What do I have to lose?

Selim made up his mind that he would never go back and plead for help. Instead, chin high, he strode across the dunes as far as he could. He would rather die than beg forgiveness from the likes of them. Ebrahim had lied to protect his own life, but Naib Dhartha had committed a far worse crime in Selim's eyes, knowingly condemning an innocent orphan boy to death because it simplified tribal politics.

Selim had excellent desert skills, but Arrakis was a severe environment. In the several generations since the Zensunni had settled here, no one had ever returned from exile. The deep desert swallowed them up, leaving no trace. He trudged out into the wasteland with only a rope slung over his shoulder, a stubby dagger at his belt, and a sharpened metal walking stick, a piece he had salvaged from the spaceport junkyard in Arrakis City.

Maybe Selim could go there and find a job with offworld traders, moving cargo from each vessel that landed, or stowing aboard one of the spaceships that plied their way from planet to planet, often taking years for each passage. But such ships only rarely visited Arrakis, since it was far from the regular shipping lanes. And joining the strange offworlders might make Selim give up too much of himself. It would be better to live alone in the desert—if he could survive. . . .

He pocketed another sharp rock, one that had been thrown from above. As the mountain buttress shrank into the distance, he found a third shard that seemed like a good throwing stone. Eventually, he would need to capture food. He could suck a lizard's moist flesh and live for just a little while longer.

As he made his way into the restless wasteland, Selim gazed toward a long peninsula of rock, far from the Zensunni caves. He'd be apart from the tribe there, but could still laugh at them every day he survived his exile. He could thumb his nose and call out jokes that Naib Dhartha would never hear.

Selim poked his walking stick into the soft dunes, as if stabbing an imaginary enemy. He sketched a deprecating Buddislamic symbol in the sand, with an arrow on it that pointed back toward the cliff dwellings. He took a special satisfaction from his defiance, even though the wind would erase the insult within a day. With a lighter step, he climbed a high dune and skidded down into the trough.

He began to sing a traditional song, maintaining an up-beat composure, and increased his speed. The distant peninsula of rock shimmered in the afternoon, and he tried to convince himself that it looked inviting. His bravado increased as he drew farther from his tormentors.

But when he was within a kilometer of the sheltering black rock, Selim felt the loose sand tremble under his feet. He looked up, suddenly realizing his danger, and saw ripples that marked the passage of a large creature deep beneath the dunes.

Selim ran. He slipped and scrambled across the soft ridge, desperate not to fall. He kept moving, racing along the crest, knowing that even this high dune would prove no obstacle for the oncoming sandworm. The rock peninsula remained impossibly far away, and the demon came ever closer.

Selim forced himself to skid to a halt, though his panicked heart urged him to keep running. Worms followed any vibration, and he had run like a terrified child instead of freezing in place like the wily desert hare. This behemoth had certainly targeted him by now. How many others before him had stood terrified, falling to their knees in final prayer before being devoured? No person had ever survived an encounter with one of the great desert monsters.

Unless he could fool it . . . distract it.

Selim willed his feet and legs to turn to stone. He took the first of the fist-sized stones he carried and hurled it as far as he could into the gully between dunes. It landed with a *thump*—and the ominous track of the approaching worm diverted just a little.

Selim tossed another rock, and a third, in a drumbeat pattern intended to lure the worm away from him. He threw the rest of his stones, and the beast turned only slightly, still rising up below him.

Empty handed, Selim now had no other way to divert the creature.

Its maw open wide, the worm gulped sand and stones, searching for a morsel of meat. The dune beneath Selim's boots shifted and crumbled, and he knew the monster would swallow him. He smelled an ominous cinammon stench on the worm's breath, saw glimpses of fire in its gullet.

Naib Dhartha would no doubt laugh at the young thief's fate. Selim shouted a loud curse. And rather than surrender, he decided to attack.

Closer to the cavernous mouth, the odor of spice intensified. The young man gripped his metal walking stick and whispered a prayer. As the worm lifted itself from beneath the dune, Selim leaped onto its curved and crusty back. He raised the metal staff like a spear and plunged the sharpened tip into what he thought would be tough, armored worm-skin. Instead, the point slipped between segments, into soft pink flesh.

The beast reacted as if it had been shot with a hundred maula cannons. It reared up, thrashed and writhed.

Surprised, Selim drove the spear deeper and held on with all his strength. He squeezed his eyes shut, clenching his teeth and pulling back to keep himself steady. He would have no chance if he let go.

The little spear couldn't have wounded the demon; this was merely a human gesture of defiance, a biting fly thirsty for a sweet droplet of blood. Any moment now the worm would dive back beneath the sand and drag Selim down with it.

Surprisingly, though, the creature raced forward, keeping itself high out of the dunes where the exposed tissue would not be abraded by sand.

Terrified, Selim clung to the implanted staff—then laughed as he realized he was actually *riding* the monster! Shaitan himself! Had anyone ever done such a thing? If so, no man had ever lived to tell about it.

Selim made a pact with himself and with Buddallah that he would not be defeated, not by Naib Dhartha and not by this desert demon. He pulled back on his spear and pried the fleshy segment even wider, making the worm climb out of the sand, as if it could outrun the annoying parasite on its back. . . .

The young exile never made it to the strip of rock where he had hoped to establish a private camp. Instead, the worm careened into the deep desert . . . carrying Selim far from his former life.